I0634222

LIFE ON THE RUN
PART II

AUTHOR JOE FRAZIER

Printed in the USA

PUBLISHER'S NOTE:
This book is a work of fiction. Names, Characters, places and incidents are products of the imagination. Or used fictitiously any resemblance to actual events or locals or persons living or dead, is entirely coincidental.
Copyright © 2017 Joe Frazier
All Rights Reserved, including the right of reproduction in whole or in part of any form.
ISBN- 978-0-692-96071-4
Library of Congress Catalog Card Number: In publication data.
Life on the Run Part II
Written by: Joe Frazier
Edited by: Complete Steps Publishing, LLC
Text Formation: Complete Steps Publishing, LLC
Cover Design and Layout: Dynasty's Cover Me
Printed in the United States of America

THE SAGA CONTINUES...

"**A**min if you can hear me, can you move your fingers for me? Amin, can you hear me? Amin the house is on fire, we got to get out of here. Amin can you hear me?" Slowly, I begin to move my fingers and now I feel like I'm in a stadium full of fans after a home run or a touchdown. When I open my eyes, I get showered with disco lights from flashing news camera's, causing me to zoom in on the situation. I don't know exactly what's going on but as I'm looking around I come across one familiar face that just blew me a kiss, with a waterfall of tears running down her face. I wonder why this woman is crying. But the longer I stared, I'm slowly realizing that woman is my mother. So now, I'm watery eyed and filled with mixed emotions. Everything is coming back to me and now I realize these cock-suckas done caught me anyway. My hands and feet is handcuffed and everybody is just staring at me. Including the Doctors. I guess they sizing up how responsive I am.

"Amin, do you know where you are?"

"Yes."

"Do you recognize anybody here in this room?"

"Yes."

"Who? And if it's painful to move your fingers see if you can turn in their direction and point your lips out at them."

When I pointed my lips out at my mom she fell out laughing. I guess I had a dumbass look on my face or something. She has always been silly.

"Ok Amin, the detectives are on their way to talk to you. They have been calling about you every other day. You have been in a coma for a whole year and a half. You are so blessed."

"Nurse I notice I have a bag on my side. Will I be able to use the bathroom regularly?"

"Yes, we had to put that on you because you were unresponsive with other eternal damages and it shocks the hell out of me that you're still normal. Do you know why you are in the hospital?"

"Yes."

"Did a female jump off the roof with you?"

Watching as her eyes drop to the floor. I already know her answer is not a good one.

"Yes."

"Unfortunately, Amin, she didn't make it. Was that your girlfriend?"

"Yes."

"Were you the only person she was sexually involved with in the last past six months?"

"Yes. Why so many questions Doc?"

"Just asking, By the way you're in Jefferson Hospital. If you need me just press the button and I will come, I'll give you some privacy to talk to your mom and remember detectives are on their way."

"Ok, thank you."

"Amin what happened baby? How are you feeling? Are you ok?"

"Yes."

"Now have you lost your got damn mind?"

"No, why you say that mom?"

"What made Y'all jump off the roof Amin? Wait a minute; not a house but the fuckin roof of a hotel nigga; I hope you ain't smoking that shit."

"Mom chill."

"Ok, but you know not to get Gangsta right?" We do have that understanding am I correct?'

"Mom, I'm already fucked up."

"I know baby; I'm just waking you up. But damn I guess Y'all wanted to die together huh? I bet that was the plan wasn't it?"

"Yup."

"Well damn that pussy must've been sent by an angel. Done made my son jump off a fucking roof."

"Mom can you stop."

"No son, I'm just saying I know the difference between basic pussy and that pussy that comes with a warning sign. Basic pussy is that kind of pussy that don't be on your mind all the time. You can fuck basic pussy thinking about who you hope win the football game. But that pussy that come with instructions, you most definitely need to read the instructions nigga. Because that fuck at your own risk pussy make mothafuckas act strange. Like leaving messages on the bitch phone talking about you gone kill yourself if she don't answer her phone. Amin, you know I'm not lying because you done fucked around and jumped off a roof that was twenty-two stories high. So, you know I know you didn't read the instructions to that pussy."

"Mom, like why right now? I'm like still on my death bed and you got jokes."

"No son, I love you and now I'm scared; because I'm hoping you don't ever find no more pussy that make you feel like you can fly, you fuckin nut."

Joe Frazier

I guess sometimes you have to dig deep for understanding when people do things out of the ordinary because it's definitely a reason for absolutely everything that happens and what I get out of mom's actions is she's sad and hurt that I'm in this situation and she's making memories because she knows I'm knee deep in some bullshit and neither one us is sure if I'm ever getting out of it.

Out the corner of my eye I see the suits and ties casually entering my room and I like how they're patiently waiting for my mom to notice them so she can excuse herself. But knowing her, she already knows who they are and why they're here. But acting like they're insurance men.

"Amin Gibson?"

"Yes"

"I'm Homicide Detective Marsh Shallow and this my partner Mr. Kevin McKinney and wait a minute is this a family member or?"

"Umm yes, I'm his Mother can I take your order?"

"Ma'am I'm afraid you can because we have an order to arrest your son for capital murder and robbery with related offenses that's pending investigation. Now can you put an extra Coke with my shit?"

My mother just flopped down on me hugging me tight as she could, crying like she's looking over top of me in my casket. She's bleeding pain into my emotions. I'm fighting back tears hard as I can, I never heard my mom cry like this.

The nurse walks in with papers in her hand headed straight to my bed.

"Amin, can you sign where the x is these are your release papers."

Life on the Run

Knowing that I'm going with these detectives gave me the twilight creeps. But I already know it's a band full of music I have to face and take responsibility for. But it is what it is I guess.

I don't know how my life got sent in this direction. I feel like I'm on a highway to hell. As if something is remote controlling my decisions while I'm in the passenger seat.

24-Hours Later

I'm looking like a human carrot with this orange jumpsuit on. As I'm getting booked and processed and receiving my sheets and care package, I see a big sign that says, "BREAK THE LAW YOU MEET NEW FRIENDS" Whelp, it's looking like I have more friends than I asked for in this motherfucker. Some look happy to be here and some look like they wish they never did that shit. I guess I go over there and chill with them.

I'm on D-2-3, where all the violent criminals live. So the first impression must be confident and comfortable. If you walk into a curious zone nervous you become a person of interest.

"Ok you're in cell 30 top bunk Amin."

Shit, all eyes on me as I bop to my cell. I broke my ribs and legs and healed up while I was in the coma. I'm sore as hell, my legs are skinny, and I feel funny. This crazy. I'm down to 120 l.bs from 220 and I already know they don't feed you shit in here.

I walk up on my new cellmate and stick my hand out for a shake.

"Hey what's good, I'm Amin."

"Hey fella they call me Kay. What it is my nigga?"

"Shit I can't even tell you right now big homie, this some bullshit."

"You telling the truth so far."

"Well you can expect me to be a straight up and down ass nigga from here on out. I might can't tell you everything but at least I won't lie to you."

"I like that. I just have my own way in nipping shit in the bud in the beginning so a nigga wouldn't even feel comfortable bringing me some bullshit. You feel me Amin?"

"I got you Kay."

SIX MONTHS LATER

Time had passed and the block has flipped around. Niggas went home, 1 to the up-state, drug programs and the hole during shakedowns. I done got broken in a bit. I got me a job wiping tables and sweeping on the block but the part I'm not feeling is that these niggas think I'm a damn mail-man. Always calling me to do them a favor. I cut that shit short early so now when a nigga pumps himself-up to ask me, either they got a snack for me or they got the most innocent puppy look on their face, like they'll appreciate it from the bottom of their heart. People is so friendly when they want something. Boy, I tell you. But what I'm learning is that you never put trust into a smile. Shit, I even smile back, just to keep it flowing. But people put on a whole new mask when they in need. If I had an extended way of thinking at the time, I would've just went to school knowing at the end of the day my mind would've been more advanced, instead of worrying about what people said about me. So I guess it took me to become knee deep in some shit I can't get out of to become a leader in my life. Knowing that if I walk alone it wouldn't matter if I was lonely. All because I know once I get to where I'm going, everybody there is already on the same page I'm on. And just by gaining that kind of mentality it easily helps me spot a dumbass nigga from far away.

"Amin I done fuck around and came up on some onions and green peppers, cheese and some more shit. This Chi-Chi going to be a classic later on. And my bad I just pulled you out of a deep zone, you were really somewhere else my nigga."

"It's all good just collecting my thoughts you feel me Kay?"

"I feel you my nigga. A nigga that take time to think is going places in life because it's most definitely mind before action youngin."

"You ain't never lied. But you said you got what for the Chi-Chi my nigga? You done fucked around and made me hungry."

"Well shit I got a small treat in the cut just chill till I get off the phone."

"Ok, but don't get on the phone and start reminiscing about shit you did when you were little right?"

"Amin, you funny as shit."

When people found out who I was and what I was locked up for, due to a dick eating ass correctional officer, I got my props, respect and a lot of unwanted attention.

Kay is off the phone now and his whole demeanor is different from when he first got on the phone. I can always tell when something is fucking with somebody. Especially, when they try to play it off like everything good.

"What's up my nigga everything good?"

"Hell naw! I'm glad you somebody I can talk to because I just caught on to some fucked up shit."

"What it is then?"

"Look at you Amin you nosey as shit, already"

A burst of laughter came in between the conversation.

"So ok, so I call my crib and I guess my son pressed the right button and excepted the phone call. So in the background I hear my little brother arguing with my bitch on some, where she been type of shit. So at first, I'm taking it like she had him babysitting and she probably made a couple extra runs or whatever. But I actually heard this bitch tell my little brother to stop taking her so serious. Because she fuck with me and she can fuck whoever she feels like when she want to. So I'm waiting for the part where she sees my son got the phone and come say hello. See I heard that shit so bam, it hit me that my little brother really got feelings for my baby mom like wow am I really hearing this shit? I left this nigga my connects, a half a brick and seven pounds of loud. So he's seeing them digits I was seeing. So I guess he feeling Gucci. I'm not going to lie Amin; my baby mom is tough. Like this bitch should be a model. I let this bitch ass nigga live with me when his bitch put him out and this son of a bitch been with me ever since. So my girl got a little comfortable around him I guess. Coming downstairs in them short shorts with that fat ass looking all sexy. I lie to you not, I fucked this bitch every five minutes when we first started kicking it. I want this nigga out my house and far away from me before I fuck around and kill his punk ass. I always wondered if he looked at my bitch in that way, imagining shit and having all kinds of sex with her in his head. You know how we see a bad bitch then the next thing you know you fucking her like this. Like that on demand deep throats and don't front like you don't have that special space in your mind where you be fucking the shit out of bitches' nigga."

"Damn so your little brother done fell in love with your baby mom Kay?"

"My nigga, that's what it sounds like. This shit got me ready to take a deal just to get out there and beat the brakes off this nigga. I give him street safety and credibility and wow this the thanks I get. That comes in a form of fuck you. Life is crazy. I won't ever do any nigga a favor like that again. So Amin, make sure you stay on your feet because you aren't bringing your ass in there either."

"Well shit in that case you have to blame both. Because that type of shit goes through a process of flirts. So if she never put that nigga in his place then she wasn't shit in the beginning Kay."

"I know but you know how we fall for these pretty bitches Amin. Anything they say, we just believe it. All because we satisfied that the bitch, even having a conversation with us, you feel me Amin?"

"Hell yeah! Especially, when you single."

A moment of silence just crept in the cell as we both fell in deep thought. I don't want to say nothing to him to distract him from unraveling his situation. I know that's more painful than anything. Especially, because he locked up.

"You know what Amin? You know what really had me wanting to get rich at an early age?"

"I'm listening"

"Check this out, my mom met this drunk ass nigga when I was like ten and I guess this drunk ass nigga took over the bills or whatever. So since he did all that, I guess he felt like he can say and do whatever in the house. So my mom basically went for the shit. Me, I'm just looking lost and helpless. So as time passed by, I grew up a lil bit. I hit the streets and found me a connect for the paper and got on and got on good. I came across my players in the street and then I molded me a team of killers. Just waiting for a fuck nigga to act up. One day my mom come running out the house and this drunk ass nigga come walking behind her talking some gangsta shit. I thought about how much money I had in my stash and at that time. I had about thirty-thousand, so two months later, I bought my mom a crib and didn't tell her until it was renovated. When I told her I was hoping she would be happy, I got her a crib in the suburban area in the northeast out there by Franklin Mills Mall. So when I told her she was lit up in disbelief. I already knew he thought he was going with her but I also knew that she didn't need him no more because she only had to pay taxes at the end of the year. I was hoping he tried to bully his way in my mom new house, just so I can catch him on a dark street and blow his drunk ass into his dreams. But he fucked around and got killed six months later anyway. He started arguing with these niggas in the bar, talking some killa shit to these niggas that love to buss they guns and they waited for that nigga to come outside and shot him seventeen times."

"Fuck outta here. Y'all niggas did that shit you trying sound like the nice guy in the situation. You funny as shit Kay."

"Amin ol 'head be buggin. I used to trip off him then it got to the point where his shit wasn't funny no more but you know everybody got they own problems."

"Damn hearing that got me sitting here looking at how everything was taken from me all at once. My main man, Damien, then my girl I just fell in love with and my freedom."

"When it rains, it pours my nigga."

"Ok I'm going to sleep Amin. Because you swear you gonna burn my ears out. Nope, not tonight you won't."

ONE YEAR LATER

"AMIN GIBSON OFFICIAL VISIT!"

"AMIN GIBSON OFFICIAL VISIT!"

Damn after a whole year and some change a lawyer just now coming to see me. "Yes, I'm Amin Gibson?"

"Let me see your armband."

"Ok go to room 325. Your lawyer is here and if your lawyer isn't there wait till they come."

"Ok'

As I'm walking down the hallway anxiety comes from out of nowhere as I become fearful of what this lawyer has to say. I feel like I'm walking straight to the death chambers.

As I reach room 325 I become face to face with a tall Arabian, curly haired fella. Automatically, I'm feeling like he's going let them hang me.

"Hello my name is Hassan Rassin and I'm here to update you about your case here. Amin, right? Did I get it, right?"

"Yes."

"Ok Amin I have some good news and some bad news so we're going to start with the good news. Now this is what's happening here, your buddy Diamond, you remember her right?"

"Yes."

"Ok, well she had a conversation with her mother before she died and inside that conversation Amin, she told her mother that nobody knew what she was up to until the last minute. Her mother, Ms. Angel appeared at a Preliminary hearing and took the stand

and her statement of what happened and how it happened basically worked in your favor. It explained that you were not aware of what was going on and you didn't know Diamond's intentions. You didn't take part of any crime so the courts want to know if you want to plead guilty for receiving stolen property. Diamond and Karen shoplifted clothes for you and you excepted it right?"

"Yes."

"Well that's it for the good news. You will be cleared of all charges for the homicide as well."

"So now here's the bad news. You ready Amin?"

"Just get to it please."

"Ok do you remember talking to a dude named Camargo Sims?"

"Camargo?"

"Amin come on I don't feel like this shit. You remember the dude Cargo, Karen introduced you to, right?"

"Yes, I do."

"Ok the A.T.F missed you by inches leaving the house out Baltimore, MD. They had been watching for one, Cargo been under surveillance. Cargo tried to turn somebody in before he turned himself in. To go straight in and lay on a soft pillow. Amin the Feds found 75,000 in cash, and a street value of one million dollars in heroin, three kilos of cocaine and four semi-automatic weapons with homemade extended clips. Which is a whole different charge and for all that you can get enough months to add up to the rest of your life. So what do you have to say about this?"

"So basically, you're telling me Cargo is throwing crime in my jacket?"

"Amin that's exactly what I'm saying. So what do you have to say about this? Because these type of situations is no different than a domestic violence case where she says you hit her and they lock you up and you have to prove that you didn't. Are we on the same page here Amin?"

"Yes, we are but what the fuck."

"Well you didn't deny it. I guess you take responsibility then."

"Don't put words in my mouth prick. Would you like if I put a gun in yours?"

"They take the guns at the gate Amin. But anyway, what's the reason for your silence in this situation?"

"Where I come from, after you done told on a nigga, you not safe no more. You become no different from the target at the gun range."

This Lawyer is now looking me deeply in my eyes and as I hold sturdy eye contact with him, I see pure evil in him.

"Well it sounds like you follow the rules when it comes to the streets so you make me feel like you have a blend of loyalty flowing through your veins. Am I wrong?"

"No, you're actually right."

"Well this situation isn't bad as it seems Amin."

"The fuck you mean bad as it seems? If I'm found guilty on these crazy ass charges I'm gone forever."

"Like the FUCK I said, it isn't bad as it seems."

"Well shit tell me some news I can use then."

"Ok well let me ask you a question. Would you put your life on the line to get out of here if you had the chance Amin?"

"If I got found guilty on these charges, you damn right. Because you can't enjoy life in jail."

"Ok, what if I did you a favor? Would you be able to return a favor Amin?"

"What you sending a girl to my cell for some hanky panky?"

"No, I have freedom."

As I look in his eyes I see there's no sign of betrayal on what he just told me. But where exactly is this shit going.

"Ok well let's get to it what's the favor in return?"

"It's all beneficial, that's all you need to know for now but before I leave I need to know if we have a deal or not?"

"Yes, we have a deal?"

"Enough said now. One thing you need to remember from here is that if you ever tried to back out on me you will disappear faster than your last two footsteps. Are we clear little buddy?"

"We Clear."

"So, listen, when you come home you can't return the favor right away because a deal for probation is waiting for you for being in the wrong place at the wrong time. So in between time, until your probation is over, I'll have a house for you that's all yours and a Cadillac truck for you to get around in. The truck you have to pay me back for. But this conversation stays here because telling somebody is like backing out to me. More than likely it would throw me under the bus. Now one thing you need to remember is that you got some fucked up charges and have no paid lawyer and no explanation to get you out this shit. So this is between us until you die are we clear?"

"You damn right."

"Ok, now you can expect a public defender to come offer you a deal and you already know to turn him down and you also can tell him to kiss your ass so… feeling a lil better Amin?'

"Hell yeah."

"Ok I will see you soon and you're welcome."

"Thank you I most definitely appreciate it."

Walking back to the block I got a whole different set of emotions getting around my system, I got a nice lil stroll with my shit. I'm the fuckin man right about now but damn how about this lame ass Cargo. I told Karen I wasn't feeling him. Now look, the shit I felt like he could do, he fucked around and did it. So now if I ever see that nigga, I'm a blow his new ideas out his fuckin head, but I'm wondering what happened to the coke we had at the hotel. They either kept that shit or somebody picked it up and kept it moving. I can't get over this chump Cargo. I bet if Karen was alive, she probably kill his phony ass herself. Niggas that can't turn down sex, be the easiest ones for murder.

I felt funny in the very beginning about this nigga. This shit hurt me and now I see you can't trust nobody in the game. Not even the nigga you are grabbing that shit from.

Going back on my block I see everything on lock again, for what I don't know, but shit, whatever I got to do for this strange ass lawyer or whoever he was I'm all for it because this some stressed out shit right here.

As I'm going in my cell my cellmate got this smirk on his face for whatever reason.

"What it is homie what happened?"

"Kay this public defender ass nigga just tried to offer me 50-100 years. I know you can tell by the look on my face he had me fucked up right?"

"Wow, like no thinking about how he can break shit down or curve some shit just take it or leave it Amin?"

"A Kay man, this shit crazy."

"Amin that's just why I be looking at them broke ass gangsters like how you a killer with no fuckin money for lawyers and bail. All they want is the hood to know that they shot or killed somebody then get in here looking like they was strung out on drugs because ain't nobody showing no love. Just seeing that, it don't even matter how many bodies a nigga got away with. Let a broke ass thug ever come at me with some dumb shit. I guarantee you, I make the news. I can't stand impatient, broke-minded, ass niggas, talking about let me hold something. These Niggas-Boy. I tell you."

"Damn all I said was he offered me 50-100 and you just went in on the streets Kay."

"No, because this some serious shit. We done got all cool and shit and the thought of never seeing you again is depressing. You one cool dude and I don't fuck with everybody, if you was a sucka I would've found me a book to read or be knocked the fuck out on lock down. This combination helps time fly my nigga. But while you was on your visit the little stocky nigga tried me in the chow line on some loud shit. I let him win because I knew he just got seven-ounces of weed in. So, I waited till after we ate and watched him go to his cell. Amin, he was giving me the look like he was calling me a bitch ass nigga under his breath. So as he's going in his cell, I go to our cell and got my knife and ran up in that nigga cell and locked myself in and started asking that nigga where the weed was. He started acting retarded so I whipped this long ass knife out, grabbed him and stabbed him in his face and asked him again. He still didn't want to give it to me so I stabbed him in his leg. The knife got stuck so I started punching him in his face. Eventually, he gave in. Now by that, time blood was everywhere. All on my hands. I was flat out suspect that's why they locked the block down and I don't know when they coming to shake the block down. But I got a mean stash spot so what I'm about to do is roll us a fat ass blunt and chill you down?"

"Like four flat tires my nigga."

"That's why I fuck with you Amin."

20

Life on the Run

It's funny that I'm really growing a heart for this nigga Kay. I barely know him but it's like some kind of chip people can put in your emotions that gives you an accurate feeling. If their good peoples or not in the very beginning. But at the end of the day, I'm glad I have that recognition because sometimes you can be with all the wrong people and don't even realize it. But if they came into my life it's something I need to learn from them. Either a blessing or a lesson. Something they might say can trigger good thoughts and ideas or either their ways can give me an upgrade on how I carry myself or either you come in contact with the demon that questions your curiosity for evil doings.

But as I live and learn I see that it's millions of people that think the same way I do. But has a different outcome on decisions. At one time, I thought that if a person came from a wealthy home that intelligent planning would be inherited. But I was wrong about that too. I notice I came across people that came from happy homes that turned out to be certified fuck up's. Sometimes I wonder if some people get so overwhelmed by jealousy, that they choose to tear themselves down to be equal. All because they didn't know how to show love from up top. It just makes me wonder because if you came from a peach how the fuck did you turn into a lemon? I guess fear plays a part to. Me, I don't give a fuck who's jealous and when it comes to fear we are born equal, these mothafuckas got a death switch on their lives just like everybody else and…"

"Damn that shit must've hit you hard my nigga."

"Lol why you say that Kay?"

"Because I sat and watched you zone out for a whole fucking hour. You in your thinking bag bitch."

"As I should."

Joe Frazier

"No Amin, this one of them moments I wish I had my phone to record you. If you could've seen how you was just looking, dumb as shit staring at the wall my nigga. I'm talking about like, when a crack head just took a bump my nigga."

A hard laugh just broke out and damn it feels good, I'm holding my stomach because I'm laughing so hard this shit hurt. I fuck with this nigga.

I see this weed got him fucked up too because he still smiling after a whole three minutes. At the end of the day, I most definitely fucks with him. He's normal after fucking somebody up like that. I guess it's a whole different emotion when a nigga deserves it. I'm in agreement with it. Shit, so if homie want revenge I guess we got recreation. When you go looking for trouble sometimes you find more than what you were looking for.

Two Weeks Later

Looking stranded, standing on the top tier looking down at how the block is moving. I'm just noticing how niggas that's past forty is mingling with the younger crowd and automatically I see in them a lack of wisdom. Not because I see them mingling, it's because I see it's a normal routine.

To my surprise a correctional officer sneaks up on me while I'm in my zone.

"Excuse me sir but you can't be lingering on this top tier. Either you in your cell or down in the day room. And look me in my face because my crouch didn't say nothing to you."

"Well your pussy print got my attention and it automatically put me in a state of mind of sex. You knew what the fuck you were doing when you put them tight ass pants on. Now why you teasing me?"

"Well I like how you so up front with how you really feel."

"What's your name C/o? Oh Ms. Rodriguez. Don't take it all serious love, this just me baby no offense but if you want to get to know me it might as well be real from right here. I'm attracted to pretty women. But loyal, once I make a commitment."

"I see you got some shit with you already."

"No, how about I'm gonna be me where ever I go so do you feel advanced?"

That fast-little shy smirk that just slid across her face just told me it's something she likes about me. I'm only speaking my mind. Shit, how can you land right if your sky diving ain't right. If I didn't learn nothing else, it's all about how you deliver yourself into somebody's personality that makes you valuable or useless because we most definitely got some bird brains among us.

"You on them fuck it kind of niggas I assume huh?"

"Baby all I can be is me I can't give you no more."

"Why are your eyes watering?"

"Because we didn't ask to come here and just to come through this way I'm not sure if I'm ever going to see the streets again."

"Well what can I do to help you mentally, besides sucking your dick and sneaking you off to fuck me?"

"I need some money because I lost everything with nobody to depend on."

"Well are you sentenced or still going through your court shit?"

"I'm still in the ring baby I don't know the outcome of this shit?"

"Well I'm going into nursing soon so I can put like four thousand dollars on your books just to hold you. At least I will feel comfortable walking off knowing I blessed somebody if I never see you again."

"I get the feeling you just told me some bullshit."

"Just have a seat and enjoy the ride. I said what I said now I have to go because this is looking too personal."

As Ms. Rodriguez walks off, I see she got one of them asses with that lump that makes you want to fuck her in every place where nobody's looking. Then the shake she putting in the walk got me ready to come at her on some between me and her type shit. Since she so generous. All this shit is strange to me "sheesh."

When Karen crosses my mind it's just a sad moment because all the laughs and jokes with reading between the lines of some funny shit brought us closer than people that been together over thirty years. Remembering how that pretty face used to wrinkle up when I'm all the way up in her. How can I forget. I don't know who I owe apologies to or who to give my condolences to because damn, we clicked in first gear and just took off. I loved Karen because I felt the truth in her attraction for me and for who I was. That shit felt better than bussing a big nut in the best pussy in the world.

When I think about Diamond I remember how talented she was when she had my dick in her mouth and my question was, was she just a freak or was she trying to get me sexually attracted to her. Because I couldn't become more aggressive with her ponytail gripped in my hand, shoving her head against my stomach causing my nuts to slam into her chin. I was like damn she really let me do all that. Oh shit! I guess she wanted more. The only thing that allowed me to do so was the fact that we all had a destination of a point of no return riding on a express train to a fucked up life. Shit, I needed all the memories I can get knowing it's over once they caught us. Looking over my shoulder here comes Kay and he got one of them strolls that makes me feel like he's in a good mood, this nigga makes me feel like he's an unforgivable killer sometimes. It's just the vibe in his demeanor that provides definition, but if people love people that they can relate to, do they get a sense of how you really are that makes them comfortable dealing with you in the beginning or can they just read it in your eyes when they look at you.

"What's up baby boy, you good?"

"Yeah Kay man. I'm taking it as it come. How you?"

"I'm good you know I talked to my mom and she told me some crazy shit my uncle did?"

"Fuck Unk done did now?"

"Amin Unk done broke in the back door and stole the lil chicken she had in the oven and it had to be hot as a motherfucker because she seen him switching hands running down the streets from the 2nd floor window. I don't want to kill my family but this is my mom they playing with. You know we don't get no picks when it comes to mom. I can just picture the smoke coming off the chicken while he switching hands. He do some real Three Stooges shit sometimes man."

"Aye Kay, I would've been on the floor cracking the fuck up."

"Amin It seem like soon as I got locked up all this bullshit started happening. Then this trash ass baby mom I got showing her ass because I can't just say we out on some world tour shit and unpredictable spending missions so now I see what her true love really fell on. What can I do for her, like she just a fucking kid? They not always hoes. Amin, they sometimes not mature enough to level up to your understanding and how you see shit. Everybody not on your level and not to say I'm perfect but man we living in a selfish world. I didn't have to share a damn thing. But then again you supposed to share and wish a bitch ass nigga would think I'm sweet."

"Kay we already living in a world of betrayal. So what the fuck did you really expect from this girl? Every nigga or every chick don't have what it takes to get up on that thinking level when it comes to being financially stable. So I look at it like it's either you love her to the point she feels comfortable and satisfied with you, or wait till she starts doing dumb and dumber shit, being their friend first makes it all about you."

"You smoked something without me nigga?"

"Naw. why you say that?"

"Because you talking some real good shit and you got me thinking different. Let me check my stash nigga."

Silence arrived in the cell and here I am in wonderland again. If this is not a sad way to live, I don't know what is. What gets me the most is noticing how happy and comfortable some of these dudes are in here or should I step in their shoes and notice how they made the best out of a fucked-up situation.

I miss Karen so much to the point tears fall down my face without me feeling my eyes watering. It just comes. I wonder if Kay hear my silent cries some nights and just automatically understand that this is painful. I get cramps about it when I think about her too long, it's a difference between not speaking to somebody again from not being able to ever speak to them again. Life has so many surprises.

The closer I get to my court date the more nervous I'm becoming because deep down I feel like this the last chapter of my life. Out of everything that happened, I be lucky if I get a life sentence or should I just bank on what Mr. Hassan said? Fuck it, I'm going to sleep. This shit crazy.

THREE DAYS LATER...

"Amin Gibson report to the front desk"

"Amin Gibson report to the front desk"

Shit it's too early for this. As I'm leaving my cell heading down the stairs I see Ms. Rodriguez. When we catch eye contact, I notice she's fighting for the grin not to appear on her face but what the fuck is this about.

"Good Morning Ms. Rodriguez."

"Good Morning Amin, umm listen I need to speak with you so put on your blue shirt and meet me in the doctor's area. A pass will be waiting on you when you're ready."

"Ok I'll be there."

Damn I wonder if she really kept it decent. If she did, then what did I do to deserve all this.

All eyes on me as I'm headed back towards the front and it's all correctional officers. I know I got a crazy case but it's a lot of criminals in here with much more seriousness to their cases but anyway here we go.

"Well here I am in my blue shirt Ms. Rodriguez."

"Ok Amin listen; I'm going to be leaving Tuesday for good. But I kept my word I did a little more than I said I was. But anyway, you'll be moving to another block, a much more laid back block Okay?"

"Ok but when will I be moving? And why am I moving? And what did I do to deserve all these blessings from you?"

"Amin, you live and you learn. You most definitely will see me again young buck."

"But Ms. Rodriguez, I'm so confused like what is going on? I ask because I just met you and you're giving me money and comforting me and we don't even know each other."

"Let me say this, we didn't meet, I came to meet you. You don't know me. But I know you. You have a court date coming up in 6 months. So when you get in the courtroom you will see me there again. I will wink at you just to put a smile on your face, the conversation we had in here stays in here so when we split up, it stays in here. You feel me young buck?"

"I feel you OG."

"No, you want to feel on me. But do you check the box and agree to the terms and conditions to me saying this is between us my nigga?"

"Yes, I check the box."

"Well okay then this went good then, I'll see you soon and stay away from violent people because if you with them then Y'all are a team. So if you kill somebody in here representing your click, then you can hang it up, because then you're never coming home. So watch who you affiliate yourself with. Now this meeting is over keep your nose clean in here Amin."

"Ok thank you Ms. Rodriguez."

"You're welcome Baby." Damn if nothing else ate me alive it's this, knowing it's something waiting for me in the dark and can't tell what it is yet. Now, I can't wait till I get in court to get this shit over with. My lawyer Hassan, with this favor shit, then here's Ms. Rodriguez with the she knows me but I don't know her. Like what the fuck is going on here.

Headed back to the block with my head down because I never felt relieved with a crazy feeling in my stomach at the same time.

When I reach my cell my heart drops to the floor because it's empty, Kay is gone and none of his belongings are here. This is the part I see I'm not going to be able to adjust to. You can't control the time a homie is there with you. To laugh, trip, and just make these days go faster.

On my bed, I find a note written by Kay.

"Damn homie, olé boy not only told on me, this punk ass nigga pressed charges on me. I will be at the police station for a couple days to see what I'm being charged with. But now that I see this shit, Amin I rather for you not to feed into none of that shit going on up in there because you don't know who gangster by blood from the actors. Some people are just frustrated looking for a chump to blow steam off of. Amin I'm living and learning right with you. I know your #pp number and will fly a kite from wherever I land…miss you already bro."

Damn this is crazy. I'm glad he went through that tunnel before I did. Now I guess I'll have to detour around the fuckery. Especially after what Ms. Rodriguez said. Just by her crossing my mind, I find it amazing how my emotions can shift from me being attracted to her to being curious of her. It's hard getting lost down lover's lane because she claimed to have kept her word. I'm more curious than ever. It's like being on that one roller coaster ride in Disney World that goes through the middle of a mountain in the dark and you don't know what's going to happen.

As I'm listening to music playing in my head and echoes from the voices shouting out on the block from their cells, to my surprise, a guard just slid some mail under my door addressed with my name on it. Here's my invitation to a judge's courtroom. She said I would be in court in six months. I see it's a lot sooner than what they said and it's for trial. Like I guess I wasn't welcome at my own preliminary hearing.

My door pops unlock and now they're calling me over the loud speaker.

"Amin Gibson report to the front."

"Amin Gibson report to the front."

When I get to the front the guard tells me to pack up because I'm moving, Ms. Rodriguez words are slowly coming to light. I see this train is beginning to take off.

The thing about this move to a new block is that I hate having to get broke into the environment all over again. But who asked me to come here? Shit!

As I'm leaving I can feel the eyes of Kay's enemy on the back of my head but it just didn't make since to act gangster. If main man wasn't no Gangster, if I didn't know nothing else, I knew these niggas was already stressed out with their own problems so the best way to play, is in your own lane. I guess he earned everything that happened to him, bitch ass nigga.

I know Kay is feeling the same way I am, when you separate two cool cellmates it's like separating twin brothers. Life is much more than what we accept.

At the end of the day I landed on a laid-back block like Ms. Rodriguez said I would. Now I have a single cell. This girl got some pull in this building I see.

Looking back at how shit made me feel, I see I got to rock off my first instinct. I swear it was something about that nigga Cargo, Karen bumped it up to be all good just because he was a ghetto superstar a while back. I already know that when niggas getting money for a long period of time it's like you can't stop it from being hot and the feds is watching niggas like we watch A&E. I damn sure couldn't tell Karen nothing about this nigga Cargo. But check me out now.

This is a lot to deal with as a young buck. I honestly feel like I missed my stop and got stuck on a high speed train headed far away from how I do things and how I would normally live my life. I'm like really in jail, in my county blues. I wish this was just a dream. I'm the last one alive and I have to pay for everything not including Eli and Diamond situation in the South. Just because I'm from Philly they would probably invite me to some kind of charges

CHAPTER ONE

Finally, I made it to the social worker. I really need to know my court date.

"Hello sir and you must be?"

"I'm Amin Gibson Ma'am."

"Oh okay I been meaning to get to you a little earlier but the warden gave me something for you to sign. Of course he didn't send it when he said he was but I have it here with me now. My name is Ms. Mason and I will be your social worker until you leave this unit. This is a check, in the amount of ten-thousand dollars but the courts have a lien on a portion of this check, due to court fees and fines. Are you okay with that Mr. Gibson?"

"Yes I am."

"Well okay I will write you a pass to come check back with me so you can check your balance. Wait a minute sir, I believe you have a court date coming up this week for trial. You have a speedy trial. Did you ask for any of this? These are some serious charges you have here Mr. Gibson?"

"Ms. Mason I can't tell you what's going on right now. This feels like it's so out of my control. At this point I'm just awaiting a surprise landing from this situation."

"Well get ready because this Tuesday October 25th, 2013 you will find out if your landing or crashing. Just keep your head up and allow the judge to look you in your eyes so he can see the remorse I'm seeing. Because that's important and you can't hide it.

So make sure you get some good eye contact from him and here sign right here."

"Ok but Ms. Mason what charges are pending on me?"

"Mr. Gibson, you really want me to tell you something you already know? Or do you want to see if anything additional has been added to the heavy cocaine and homicide charges?"

"Well shit you just told me what I was curious about so I guess I'll be back soon to check my balance."

"I guess you will Mr. Gibson."

Damn, she said heavy cocaine charges, I guess they did find everything. Fuck it I'm just ready to get it over with.

I'm up early in the morning headed to the sink to get it together. As I reach for my toothpaste I notice a piece of paper at the bottom of my door. When I open it up I fall head first in disbelief because now I see I have an available balance of $7,500 Ms. Rodriguez must want me to tear that ass up when I get out of here. As beautiful as she is, a man would probably spend $7,500 on an average night out just to be an option. So here we go again with the same question why, why, why, I go to court tomorrow and oh my goodness I need a miracle.

It's 6:30 Tuesday, October 25th, 2013 the day I been waiting on and at the same time wishing it never came. My heart is beating hard and fast and it seems as if everything is on its way to go completely wrong.

Getting on the bus for court I'm shackled as if I shot thirty cops, wounded fourteen civilians, and ran over seven kids. I'm feeling as if I'm about to get sentenced to Hell. Damn near everybody on this bus is looking out the window fascinated with the pretty faces and fat asses. As I'm looking out the window everything seems like a dream that's never coming true. I'm feeling all sad. Especially, since my mom never once came to see me. I'm pretty sure she won't be in this courtroom when I get in there. It's crazy that I can tell the difference between who got auto theft and received stolen property charges because the seriousness that sits on a criminal face. The laughy jokey type dudes in a situation like this wasn't making no noise on the streets because everything is a joke to them in here. But the hard case niggas be straight faced in a zone letting it all go on like it's not even happening.

Pulling up to the garage doors of the courthouse, I am one nervous hand sweating nigga. If I get out of this I might start going to church because I'm scared of this time they given out down here. Before I can even make it to my cell I already hear my name being mentioned on the sheriff's walkie talkie.

"Amin Gibson step up to the door please."

"Amin Gibson".

"Here I am sir."

"Ok stand on the wall. We're taking you straight up I think your lawyer wants to speak with you

ONE HOUR LATER

"Okay Amin it's show time live at the courthouse are you ready?"

"Yes, I'm ready for this to be done and over with."

"Ok, well just remember you're all ears. You say nothing we say everything, deal?"

"Deal."

"Well we're in there next. So keep it calm for me, deal?"

"Mr. Hassan if I sign one more deal with you what am I going to become?"

"A free man. Anything else sir?"

"Not at all."

"I Didn't think so." Well he seems confident about this going good for me so I guess I shouldn't worry but so much. Wow today we really find out. As I'm looking into space, I settle into deep thought and then I'm distracted by a deep voice calling my name out.

"Amin Gibson, court. Amin Gibson, court"

OH SHIT, HERE WE GO!

Headed into the court room I'm halted by a tall Caucasian male with rookie written all over his face. This must be the lawyer Hassan was telling me about but if he's my lawyer, who the fuck is Hassan? See this the shit that got me confused because I didn't order no dream team. But since I was told by Hassan not to listen to him, everything he just said to me sounded like it was in slow motion. Now in the court room this public defender's seat is next to where I'm supposed to be seated and Hassan is standing in the District Attorney's position. So Hassan is the D.A and whoever this guy said his name is, is really my actual lawyer so what the fuck is going on here once again.

"ORDER IN THE COURT, ORDER IN THE COURT, JUDGE GREGORY SMIT

PRESIDING!"

JUDGE: "Mr. Amin Gibson will you stand and raise your right hand and state the truth nothing but the truth so help you God?"

"Yes, I do your Honor"

"Mr. Gibson, do you understand the seriousness of the charges that has been brought up against you far conspiracy to capital murder which carries up to a maximum sentence of death, or a minimum of a natural life sentence of incarceration along with the Rico Act of representing organized crime that comes with extended criminal penalties? You also have been charged with having a deadly weapon in your possession which is a 40-glock semi-automatic weapon without a license?"

"Yes, I do"

Hassan: "Your honor these Charges has been excused at the preliminary hearing due to his misunderstanding and lack of knowledge of the intensive intentions of the company he applied himself to during an unexcused absence on his first day of school."

JUDGE: "Ok Mr. Gibson if you don't mind may I ask the reason you refuse to be present on the very first day of school?"

"Your honor the bills in my home at the time was in competition with the things I was supposed to have at the time. So since first things first in this life whatever I needed came last. But the previous year before this terrible nightmare I was soaked in shame due to my appearance so since it was like a repeat I was afraid to attend."

JUDGE: "Ok well one thing I'm seeing here is drug charges that hasn't been completely excused, Mr. Gibson. The Rico Act has been excused but the charge of conspiracy of manufacturing with the intent to deliver is still alive in this matter, which you agreed to plead guilty in exchange of a sentence of five years of non-reporting probation, are you aware of this agreement?"

As the Judge ask me about the agreement I made, out the corner of my eye I can see my so-called lawyer Hassan communicating with the judge with his body language. To find out his true identity in court, I wondered why he said nothing when I was supposed to be the silent one. Fortunately, he was right, now I wonder what the fuck is this favor I supposed to return back.

JUDGE: "Mr. Gibson did you hear me correctly?"

"I'm sorry your Honor. Yes, I do understand the agreement I made."

JUDGE: "Were you threatened or did anybody force you to make the decision you made? "It's now or never"

"No, nobody threatened me or forced me into making this agreement your Honor."

JUDGE: "Ok well you are to be released immediately from the county jail. You report to your probation officer within one week of your release."

Right after the Judge made his announcement about me getting released I can hear the anger coming from the parties of the victims in the background with their comments about the system not being fair.

"Thank you your Honor."

The Judge just looks at me then calls for the next case.

As I stand up; I quickly turn around to see if Ms. Rodriguez is in Court with me but the first person I catch eye contact with is the passenger of the victim that Diamond Killed. He gives me the look of my future worst enemy. Then I lock eyes with Ms. Rodriguez and that smile she spoke about appeared on my face, cheek to cheek, I see my mother sitting in the back row but she has a mean mug, I guess she heard something she didn't like and rather them not know she's my mother. Might need to watch myself out there but knowing me, I will be that monster in real life they hate to see in their nightmares.

CHAPTER TWO

As I impatiently sit in my cell waiting to hear my name, I replay the looks and the words I heard in the court room. I know I got deep hatred from the families of the victims. I just hope they heard the part about me not knowing Diamond was going to set it off because this jail shit is not the place to be. I know I have to be strapped for that one family member that's not trying to hear that shit. It's sad but fuck was I supposed to do.

FIVE HOURS LATER

"AMIN GIBSON PACK IT UP! AMIN GIBSON PACK IT UP!" My cell door pops open and I swear I just want to bust through the walls to get out of this place. It's been damn near three years I been down just waiting to go to court. All them times I went to court and never got in and had to sit and wait until everybody had to go back to the jail. Yeah it's about that time I raise up out of here. Damn and now I get to go get me some jumbo shrimps and eat like a boss, my mind is bigger than my stomach right now. Back in my street clothes it feels so damn good to be a free man right now and I don't know how to act. But the thought of Karen not being free with me makes me feel like I don't deserve to be alive. If only we could've met from another angle, we would've been together without none of this ever happening. Diamond and

40

Life on the Run

Damien was a big loss and here I am all by my damn self. I know I have a lot of questions to answer if I ever returned back down 29th and Jefferson. So staying away will be my best choice to make.

But this Cargo nigga have some explaining to do before I empty a clip into his face or should I just let it go? He know he was wrong so he might want to take me out. Thinking, I was going to kill him anyway. One way or another I see imma have to kill him.

Finally, outside the gates listening to the never come backs and do the right things from the guards. I notice a spanking brand new all black clean Cadillac Escalade in the parking lot with the four way flashers on, with a male that fits the description of Hassan Rassin, standing on the outside of the truck. The closer I get the more I notice that's him. At this point I don't know if I should smirk, smile, laugh, or turn around and hall ass because still, what the fuck is this all about? Ok here we go, it is him.

"Hey Amin Welcome home. Now did I deliver my word to you or what?"

"Well you're definitely here waiting on me but where do we go from here Hassan?"

"Take the wheel Amin we'll discuss it all inside."

When I hopped behind the wheel I liked to shit my pants because out of nowhere a set of cold hands romantically pinched my ears from the back seat. When I turn around and look, I couldn't believe my eyes, it's Ms. Rodriguez looking pretty, dressed in her street clothes, legs crossed, fitted money green dress, black Gucci high heels, iced out chain around her neck, with a mean make up job the way she's looking into my eyes is fucking with me.

"Now Amin you are fully aware that the charges that would've kept you in jail forever not including the conspiracy of capital murder got lost, somehow right?"

"I noticed."

"Can I get a Thank you sir?"

"I most definitely appreciate it Hassan."

"Ok well that's it for today. Ms. Rodriguez will take you to your new house. This is your Cadillac truck now. I welcome you to the American Dream. See you soon and thank you in advance for returning a favor."

"Your Welcome Hassan."

Hassan gets out the truck then hops in an up to date limited edition Mercedes Benz then cruise out the parking lot playing some Jazz. Ms. Rodriguez hops in the front with a sneaky grin on her face, I almost feel intimidated by her beauty but the deep down question still stands of what the fuck is going on.

"So, Amin are you a good driver on the highway or must I take the wheel?"

"I'm good. I got a nice wheel game Ms. Rodriguez."

"You're not in jail no more. So you can call me Tina."

"Ok Tina. Tina can you explain why all this just falls in the palm of my hands?" "Well isn't it a God in heaven Amin?"

"Yes, I believe it is Tina?"

"Are you thankful that you didn't get railroaded by the system?"

"Hell yeah. That was a nightmare. Just thinking about what could've happened bothers me."

"I hear that, just having to be there for eight hours a day and sometimes more makes me feel like I'm doing a bid right with the inmates you feel me Amin?"

"I believe you. Where are we headed?"

With the clear blue skies, the sun is shining brighter than ever laced with a mild warm breeze. The smell of fresh green grass is making me love it even more that I'm out of jail. People are in short sleeve shirts. I see the white folks jogging and walking their dogs and I'm is sitting behind the wheel of a brand-new Cadillac truck with a dime piece checking me out. I know she see how these waves spinning behind this sharp ass shape up.

"So where do you want to go Amin?"

"Well I need some Seafood in my life like some crab legs, jumbo shrimps, some clams. You know the broccoli and corn type hook up. The American Dream meal. But it's another question I have to ask, I just need to get this off my chest baby."

"Baby?"

"Well Ms. Tina Rodriguez."

"No, you just sounded kind of sexy how you called me baby. You're not a shy guy are you Amin?"

"Being shy can be a turn off to some people because it kind of make people feel like they have to go through hell to get shit out of you."

"Well the shy ones be the sneakiest ones amongst us and the freakiest ones as well. Let me tell you this because I know you will be back with more questions, just know that I will answer all your questions without you asking me. I just have to size you up to get a feel on if you can really handle the answers. With that being said, it depends on you when it comes to you finding out everything or nothing at all. Enjoy your freedom and live. One thing I'm going to tell you is that riches are coming into your life. More money more problems but you are in good hands Amin."

"Good hands?" What the fuck you took insurance out on me?"

"No Asshole you're a made man now."

"Oh, shit so you're really a man?"

"Yeah, and if I am, you gon give me some of that ass. Don't play with me Amin."

Silence took over our conversation. Now all I'm listening to is the sound of the dual pipes growl like a mad pit bull as I ball down State Road. The technology in this truck is amazing.

Out the corner of my eye I can see Tina staring at me as I'm driving and it's the curious look. I'm a good actor right now because she's not even aware that I notice her. The part I don't like about this is that it's making me weak behind the fact she's here with me in this truck for whatever reason makes me feel like we might be making memories tonight.

"Amin, Cameron's on Broad Street be having them big joints, they basically got everything you need in there."

"Oh, ok well after we do the shrimps what happens after that?"

"What you want to happen after that sir?"

"The ball is in my court Tina."

"Well what your shot be like Amin?"

"Shit I'm already in the history books."

"The history books Amin?"

"Sho ya right."

"Amin after we get this Seafood you up for a couple drinks?"

"Depends on where we drinking at."

"It's a Joint called Big Bang's on Arch Street that be popping and tonight is karaoke night and I'm one of the singers. It's going to be fun. Since you with me all drinks are free."

"Must be nice."

"Yeah you might find you a nice girl down there Amin."

"Well this your spot you know who be up in here so pick me out a nice one."

"Well I let you be the judge of that one. Different strokes for different folks." Damn I'm glad this Armani shirt and Guess jeans still intact because going to a bar wasn't in my plans for tonight. It seems as if I'm getting addicted to the good life already because once she spoke about riches coming to me like everyday problems it almost made me say fuck how I return this favor as long as I get to them riches that's crazy.

CHAPTER THREE

Sitting in Big Bang's with a Long Island Ice Tea listening to how the deejay taking us back to the old school. I see this is Tina's spot. I'm glad she brought me somewhere, where people know her just in case I need to come looking for her ass for whatever reason. Karaoke starts at 11:00 pm and it's 10:45. Tina and her crew is getting ready but back and forth catching eye contact with me. I already know she representing me but I wonder how's she's doing it. Either way I guess it's a good thing.

"Amin come sit up here baby."

"Awe shit I just got shy."

I headed to the back where the girls at. I peep the flirt smirks and that's allowing me to open up a bit. If that don't it, do I bet this Long Island would.

"Hey Amin this is my home girl Sheena and this her twin sister Saleema and this her two girlfriends Kelly and Rockell. Kelly and Rockell is the backup singers, you know the blend in chorus."

"So, what are Y'all going to sing?"

"Saleema how we going to treat them tonight baby?"

"I was thinking we should do that joint by Brandy and Monica. What was the name of that song again Kelly? I was just talking about it at the house?"

"How you forget what you want to sing. I see this shit coming already. You about to get good and fucked up and think you can rap again. Don't start that bullshit tonight Saleema."

"The song was The Boy is Mine, duhh."

Life on the Run

"I know you not talking Kelly you forgot you was cooking for your man and had damn good intentions on going to the store but ended up in the casino for the rest of the night. You forgot all about he was even your man that night and till this day I still think you slid off and fucked that nigga that kept that smile on your face through them text messages. Bitch you not fooling nobody but your man."

"Ok it's about that time I guess I'll go first."

"Come on Tina you always go first."

"Bring your ass up here Saleema since you always got something to say about me going first. Now what we doing?"

"Tina let's do Fooling Around by Changing Faces."

I'm in here looking around like I'm not from this country or something. It's just women. The men out numbered. The ones that's here needed permission to come and the women is dressed to impress. The girls are looking tasty and the whole bar is waiting for their performance.

The instrumental starts to play and from the jump Tina and Saleema is so on key to the point if you made them sing behind stage you'll think the actual singers were back there.

I'm on my second, Long Island Ice Tea and all these girls is looking amazing but I'm ready to ride around the city in my new Cadillac Truck and see who down Jefferson Street. I should go around Diamond's Mother house just to give her a hug because I know she cried a river about her daughter Diamond when she was alone.

While I'm enjoying the show, out of nowhere Kelly runs up on the stage and grabs Saleema by the hair then starts to swing like a mad woman on her. Tina drops the mic and gets in between the two, getting beat up by both of them as she tries to break it up.

47

Like where is my place in this situation? I guess I'll wait to see if Tina ends up with an opponent. Then I guess I go break them up.

Big bang's done turned into a health and beauty spot because now it's all types of hair scattered around, Malaysian, Brazilian, Virgin and some more shit. Them skirts rising up and I see Saleema don't shave. I bet she don't have a problem going to the beach, relaxing her legs wide open. Wolf pussy just everywhere.

The bouncers calm the situation down and put the girls out the Bar. Tina's looking back at me with the come on Amin look on her face. But I'm not finish my drink shit that was $15.00. I will enjoy this drink by any means. The bouncer is looking at me through the glass door and I already know Tina sent for me, but his drink cost me $15.00 and I be damn if I waste my money. Saleema had no business fuckin with that girl they could've still been on stage sounding like stars. Fuck it let me down this joint and get up out of here.

When I get outside I see they're talking it out. They blowing my high with this bullshit but what puts the smile back on my face is the shine that's loving my truck. Shit, I'm just glad to be home.

"Amin I'm sorry baby I didn't know they was going to get in there and start acting like enemies, and now they cool wanting to swing with us. I know Saleema want to swing because when I told her we wasn't fucking she asked me can she fuck you so now that she know you pushing that Cadillac truck she probably wouldn't pull your dick out her mouth until you came five times. Unfortunately, we're dropping the bitch off first. She will try to lock you down. I seen something shift in her eyes when I told her we wasn't fuckin and I already know she's going to make it her business to come at you when she see you in traffic. If you fuck her just don't fall in love with her. She's a problem and love to start shit. She recently got her man locked up for beating her ass after he caught her fucking his best friend in his bed and didn't even realize he was wanted for attempted murder. So he's down for a minute. He was the bread winner and can't pay the bills from in jail. She's looking for a meal ticket to hold her down until he comes home but I don't think he's fucking with her no more. She's looking for a life like he gave her but she crossed him so you understand me a little better now?"

"Hell yeah she slimy."

"Now Amin I know you itching to see your house but it's getting late and I'm not finished getting fucked up. I got a hotel room at the Feather Nest over in New Jersey. I had for the last couple days and I want you to chill with me or at least make sure I get in safe because I know you want to go show off for the homies and let em see how you came back to the streets and all that bullshit. I still got a 5th of Grey Goose on deck and I got all the good cable channels like A&E and the joints that play hit after hit, feel me?"

"Yeah, I couldn't get into none of that while I was in jail because your back has to be turned. I just did the news. I don't have a problem chilling with you. If you don't mind me asking, do you have a man?"

"We'll finish this up after we drop them off."

Saleema, Kelly, Rockell and Sheena gets in the truck and before I can even pull off me and Saleema is catching eye contact through my rearview but after what Tina told me about her she would be the game and I would be the player. She wants to get me all alone to seduce me just to get her hands on some paper. Since I know that's her strategy I will play her own game against her and win.

Joe Frazier

Now I got that liquor in me, a truck full of bitches, I'm balling through the blocks bumping Awkward by Lil Wayne. The bass that's coming out these factory speakers put these girls right back in the club and this Saleema chick just can't keep her tongue in her mouth as she smiles at me through my rearview mirror. But first things first I'm going to Tina's hotel room and help her drink that bottle of Grey Goose to get everything I need to know out her ass because my emotions need peace. Fuck that.

CHAPTER FOUR

"**A**min this truck smell just like the seafood joint and it's really making me hungry as hell, so are you chilling with me tonight or what?"

"Well I wasn't doing shit else so did you want to stop and get something else to eat because after drinking this liquor I'm gone be ready to go in and what was the big fight about Tina that interrupted my lil groove I had going on?"

"Oh shit, see Kelly feel some type of way because Saleema's boyfriend best friend was fucking her. So when Saleema's boyfriend put her on blast for fuckin his homie it straight woke Kelly up to how her so called girlfriend really play. This nigga put her on blast on every social media he can think of and that's how Kelly found out. What confused the fuck out of me was why did Saleema play with Kelly with the song when she was the one fooling around. She always did give me a reason to believe she was half retarded because the stupid shit she do. Her boyfriend kissed the grounds she walked on. He loved that girl to the point it never crossed my mind about fucking him because that was my girl. I see she would do it to me and me telling her we wasn't fucking, was a test just to see how fast she would jump. Like fuck, if I was thinking about it or not."

"So why are they around each other then?"

"Well Kelly wasn't coming until after she found out Saleema was going to be here. I guess, I already knew something wasn't right from the look on her face when she first looked at me. Saleema didn't know Kelly knew and I damn sure didn't tell her and like Kermit none of that shit was my business. To be honest I think Saleema knew Kelly knew and didn't care because they been through worse shit than that. Shit these the same chicks that did threesomes together when they were both single and broke. So, there you have it."

I'm about due for a little snack so I'm reaching back to grab my shrimps and notice my platter is lighter than what it supposed to be so when I open it up I have four shrimps left on my platter. See now we have a problem. I'm about to turn this sumbitch around and go get to the bottom of this shit on some real loud fat boy shit. These shrimps been on my mind the whole time I was drinking. Now my shit gone and Cameron's closed now, "OH HELL NAW."

"Just bring your handsome ass in here and chalk it up."

Finally, at Tina's Hotel, I'm ready to chill. I did my taxi cab duties dropping the girls off. Now I wonder what's the next episode. I'm glad she told me all about the girls but she didn't tell me too much about Sheena. She was the quiet one that played the back. She might've been the good one that was analyzing me on the low, wondering what type of dude I was. Them the ones I like.

As Tina slides her keycard to open the door to her hotel room, all I can see is luxury and it's spacious in here. Nice big pink Jacuzzi covered with bubbles, walk-in closets, a king size bed with an extra, twin size bed. I be damn if I'm sleeping on the twin and fall out the bed in the middle of the night making all that noise hitting the floor.

"So Amin, how you like my room so far?"

"It looks like it's all yours. What made you rent a hotel? You on a business trip or something?"

"No smart ass. This is our conversational room. We can't talk business in our homes Amin. So remember that. Never on the phone either."

"I noticed. It's a lot of we & us in our conversation, lets kick it. Come on tell me some shit Tina.

"Well let's unwind first. Take this remote while I jump in the shower. Them bitches spilled drinks on me while trying to pry them apart and don't make up a reason to come in this bathroom nigga. You might see something that might excite you, Sike, just joking with you Amin."

"Well I need to take a shower too. But I don't have a change of clothes yet."

"Don't sweat the small shit baby, just crack that bottle and stop bitchin."

I hit the power button on the remote and the TV was left on a porn channel, with a threesome going on. I'm gone be smart and leave it on the porn channel and be all into it with my drink in my hand when she come out the bathroom. These Puerto Rican chicks is sexually talented. This shit got my mind on sex now. Let me turn this shit off before I get all worked up and don't get no pussy.

 Out the corner of my eye, Tina gets my attention coming out the bathroom with her new make up on and in a pink Ralph Lauren robe. I see legs so I guess she only has her panties on.

"So, ok we're going to get straight to it Amin, you do remember Hassan asking you would you return a favor if he got you out of jail right?"

"Yeah I remember."

"Ok well you remember the question about what would you do to get out of jail? And you basically said anything?"

"Yeah I remember that question."

"Ok well I'm quite sure you caught on when you went to court and seen that Hassan wasn't a lawyer. He was actually the District Attorney right?"

"Yeah that fucked my head up and my actual lawyer was lost and didn't say nothing the whole time."

"Yeah Amin Hassan and the Judge are in cahoots on a stay rich scheme and what they do is transport drugs from different Countries. They basically use their careers for a positive light to shine on their lives and when you and your crew was on the news, he looked at you as an option because he knew he could send you to jail forever. Because nigga you had a flock of charges did you see all your charges Amin?"

"No I never had a print out."

"Oh okay. See another reason you became an option was because your mother used to work for him and she was good at her shit. She used her pretty face and fitted clothes to wrap the security guards around her fingers. What fucked everything up with your mom was she caught a case in a supermarket for stabbing the cashier and had to sit for a minute."

"Wow I didn't know that. I know she did some time but that was it. Tell me what affiliated you into his way of doing things."

"Well Hassan used to live next door to me and he used to like me. But at the time I was in a relationship but we held on to small talk. Me and my friend at the time was having financial problems and things seem to get worse. To the point he used to take it out on me, because he was a broke ass nigga. He started putting his hands on me and at the same time my mother's health was failing from liver and kidney failure and her insurance didn't cover everything she needed to heal her. So I figured all Hassan could do is tell me no or he didn't have it. I asked him for a loan for Ten-Thousand Dollars

since he had the career with the life to match and then his parents
is filthy rich. To my surprise he told me he can get the money to
whoever handled the finances, as soon as possible, so mom can be
healthy again. I had to return a favor. So I ask what was the favor I
had to return and he basically told me all about what he was into.
But told me I only had to do ten trips going to Tijuana Mexico &
Afghanistan and every now & then Columbia, bringing cocaine &
heroine back into the United States. After my tenth trip, I would be
left with over a million dollars. I took him up on his offer because I
needed to get away from my boyfriend before I shot his dumb ass.
But it was strings attached."

"Well what was the strings?"

"If I told somebody and he found out I would be dead within 48
hours. Then I had to find somebody that I felt can handle the job
but when it came to you, your own mom sent him to you because
she knew you wasn't ever going to see daylight again. I left the jail
because I'm into real-estate now and doing well, and my dream
house is getting renovated. Another reason why I'm in this hotel.
Hassan told me to find you and make sure you wasn't on a
troubled block and to make it safer for you to be released without
you catching another case. So that's the most I can tell you right
now."

"So basically, I'm on my way out the country to get my hands dirty
Tina?"

"Hey, it was either that or you in jail for the rest of your life. The
reason why I'm so close to you is because I will be making them
overseas trips with you, because your mom wasn't comfortable
with you going by yourself. After Hassan paid them hospital bills
for my mother, it's nothing I won't do for him. But don't even
think about making a Career out of this because it's a dangerous
job, so get it and get out."

"Heard you loud and clear so what happen to your boyfriend?"

"Well unfortunately, while returning from an overseas trip I learned that he was shot in the head by a woman he thought he was about to have sex with. The way it was told to me, it sounds more like a hit. I honestly think Hassan made that happen because I can tell it burnt him up when I came to him after we fought. Fuck it, he's out of my life like I needed him to be."

"Well where do we go from here Tina?"

"I think you need to take a couple days to Celebrate your freedom because you dodged a hail of problems and came out a boss. So tonight we get fucked up then go shopping tomorrow and it's on me. Do you have any kids Amin?"

"Nope no kids. Tina but do you want me to stay here tonight with you?"

"Yes Amin."

"Is we Fuckin?"

"You asked me are we fucking, was that the question?"

"I see you understood me."

"What if I told you I was a dude Amin?"

"Well shit, I will be glad you told me before you cut the lights off and get naked. Now I need to do a full inspection."

"Who said we was going there Amin?"

"Look, if you a dude I have to go because you fuckin with my stomach right now Tina, or is your real name Tom?"

Tina just blew all the liquor out her mouth directly in my face from a burst of laughter.

"Let me stop. Baby I just had to check to see if you like boys because these niggas now days come in the form of a straight thug or that gangster and be gay as hell. It's so scary because, bi-sexual people catch the craziest shit. One minute they in somebody's ass then the next they in some pussy. So I had to trouble shoot you to see where your interest be. You feel me Amin?"

"Hell yeah! You scared the shit out me. I had to squeeze my cheeks together when you said that shit. I almost farted. I would've fucked this whole room up but you got me curious now on some real shit. What's good Tina?"

"Didn't you say you was taking a shower?"

"Yup."

"Ok so you'll find out when you get out and wash them boxers out because you might've shitted nigga. I do smell something that aint right in this joint Amin."

"My bad baby I did push a quiet one out."

"Ok well let me wash the system off me. I be back right after these messages."

Damn here I go again. Am I about to fall in love all over again or should I just leave? I really miss Karen and I feel like she's looking down on me. Coming out the shower I lay eyes on Tina stretched out on the bed without the Ralph Lauren robe. She is in her matching black Victoria Secret braw & panties, turning over with a shy smirk on her face. Yeah I see how this about to go. I washed my boxers out so I basically just came out strolling in my birthday suit like we been having sex for years or something."

"Amin, do I look like a dude without my clothes on?"

"Take your panties off so I can feel around for a few." I sit on the side of the bed and leaned over looking down at her love trap noticing how it's all nice and shaved, I begin to rub her and immediately she gets involved by grabbing my hand and helps me caress her love trap. We begin to lip lock and now the affection is at an all-time high. I begin sucking on her ear, easing down to her firm breast with the sound affects like she tastes so good. I'm feeding off of her reactions to my affection. I'm down in her belly button now and tonight is her night. I'm kissing my way down to her well-groomed love trap and here we go. I begin to French kissing her clit and almost immediately she came hard as Tupac when he was mad at biggie. Her good scent gave me the green light to go on a be a freak. Now it's time to get in this pussy and act a damn fool.

"Lift these legs up for me baby."

 Oh, Oh, Oahu Amin, why you, why you, oh my god you in me deep."

Watching how Tina's face is wrinkling up as I go in, is a major turn on. But I know I'm a minute man right now due to me not getting none. So I have to stretch different moves out as far as I can.

"Turn around baby."

Watching how her back just arched got me ready to bus a nut before I even get back in the pussy.

As I'm going in and out of her I'm really getting a kick out of her screams and how she's snatching the sheets off the bed, this is a good night.

"Oh, oh my god."

Damn is my ears bullshitting me or is this girl crying, damn this must be really good to her. I don't remember falling asleep but I open my eyes and it's morning, Tina's gone and I don't have a clue on where she is. I look out the window and my truck is gone but before I trip, I remember this the same chick that blessed me with that change. While sitting back up in my head Tina walks in carrying breakfast platters putting a big smile on my face. Because oh my goodness she's one beautiful woman and I can't get this little boy blush off my face for nothing in the world.

"Amin, I figured I couldn't go wrong with turkey sausage, home fries, cheese eggs, and French toast with this orange juice."

"You damn right. You couldn't and don't let nobody tell you nothing different."

"Amin I have to run out and take care some business but before I leave I can't forget to tell you that I wasn't supposed to tell you about your mom's play in this. So if you and Hassan get into a conversation, don't mention nothing about your mom. Plus, I wasn't supposed to fuck you so I have a shut the fuck up check in the top draw. I probably get to that dick again if you don't kiss and tell."

"What's the big secret Tina?"

"Hassan asked me to just make sure shit go right, nothing more nothing less."

"Oh, ok well it is what it is then."

"So, it's easy for you to not fuck me no more Amin?"

When I look in Tina's eyes I see she is serious but with a phony smirk on her face, that I can see straight through.

"Well I wouldn't say that Tina, but what I would say is that you can make this time useful and come show me how creative you are with that mouth Tina."

"So, are you asking me to suck your dick or are you asking me to cuss you the fuck out?"

"Shit I rather get my dick sucked because I heard enough profanity in jail Tina. Give me a break here."

Tina is walking towards me and I'm wondering if I bit off more than I can chew, I hope she don't want to fight, but to my surprise she gets on her knees and begin to unbutton my pants looking up at me with the freak settling in her eyes. This time I feel she is laying her mark as she French kisses this love muscle while it's half way down her throat. She knows this is something I might want again, and again and I can see me now daydreaming about this very moment when I'm alone.

CHAPTER FIVE

As I'm off on a shopping spree the only things on my mind is Macy's, Neiman Marcus and the Gucci shop; because the loafers they got make a nigga change his dress code. I noticed that damn Tina left before taking me to my house and I don't have a way to call her. So I guess I'll buy a phone while I'm out too.

As I'm mashing on the gas, catching up with the speed limit, the appreciation of freedom attacked my emotions; causing my eyes to water. Then they quickly go back to normal. When it crosses my mind that I'm headed towards a mandatory get rich or die trying episode, this favor shit is a bitch.

Finally, here at the mall and damn, females definitely got us out numbered. The Rican mommies looking so good I done fucked around and forgot why I came out here.

I never felt so alone in my life. Just going through my memories of me and Damien coming up in elementary and how much closer we became towards his unexpected death. Then Karen and Diamond. I wish she was here to suck my dick just one more time. Karen stole my heart. She really risked her freedom for me. Not having shit when she just met me. The impression of personality has more value than I thought.

THREE HOURS LATER

As I obey the speed limit I'm listening to 105.3 WDAS FM, I'm wondering when will I see Tina again. My back seats are filled up with bags. Shit, I guess I go get cute from mom's crib. I know she'll be happy to see me back in one piece.

Headed down 30th street off Girard, I see a lot of people I recognize. But I'm definitely not stopping for no small talk right now. I still feel like I got jail clothes on.

Pulling up in front of mom's house I see her and her crew sitting on the steps; drinking and having a good time. As I'm parking one of her male friends gets up off the step and tries to stop me from parking in front of my mom's door looking like he been drunk for two weeks straight.

"Yo, you can't park here. This my spot. My car is about to turn the corner from getting washed."

I ignore him and keep backing up into the parking spot. Now here comes my mother.

"Excuse me sir…Oh, shit! No, Marvin that's my baby parking! It's Ok."

Before I can get all the way out my truck moms hit me like a football player for a hug, knocking me back against the driver seat with tears in her eyes.

"Hey baby! You looking good and healthy. What that county been feeding my baby? Look at you. Hey Y'all this my Son Amin. Say hi to my baby. Come on in here let me talk to you for a minute."

"You got some money Amin?"

"Yes, I do. You need some?"

"No, I'm good. Did a female guard give you a check while you were in there?"

"Yeah Ms. Rodriguez, right?"

"Yeah what did she tell you after you came home? Because I know she linked up with you after you got out."

"Ok. But mom what's your affiliation with her?"

"It's a long story. I thought hard and fast as I could. So you did meet with the guy Hassan Rassin right?"

"Yes, we met."

"Yeah that's my work. I dealt with him before and I'm not going to lie to you it's scary as hell dealing with him. That nigga is cold hearted and take life or death chances. He respects me enough to the point, he is sending Tina that Rodriguez woman you mentioned. I think she likes you too. Did you stick your little dick in her already? Shit never mind, your facial expressions just answered my question. My only thing is Amin, if this bitch wants to jump off some shit, let that bitch jump by her damn self. To see you on the news skydiving with nothing to skydive with destroyed my soul. I couldn't believe my eyes. I have to get back out there with my company."

"Mom do you have a number for Tina?'

"Damn she might not like you all like that if she didn't give you her number. Be careful with her. Get out of this shit before you get distracted by love because I swear I don't want you to jump off another roof. Listen, you have just a couple trips to make and you're done. This won't start until your probation is up. You couldn't just walk away from all that without a leash. Do what you got to do and let it be. If you get locked up outside this country, your ass is done. So don't think about being greedy."

"Ok mom. And I won't jump off nothing else. But I need to take a shower and get dressed."

"Ok baby."

On my way to the shower, I just got to go in my room. It's memories waiting on me in there. Like that bucket of cold ass water, she threw on me, my alarm clock is still there but my room is clean with my bed made up. It's amazing how life changes in the blink of an eye.

CHAPTER SIX

Getting back in my truck after my hugs and goodbye's & see you later, I'm feeling like Mitch off Paid & Full, with the white Ralph Lauren button up, Rock & Republic jeans with the throwback Gucci's on. Honestly, I don't think they ready to see me in these Gucci loafs.

Turning on Jefferson Street, all I see is women. OK, now I need a Pepsi from out of Jimmie's. I hop out the Truck and just like I thought, all eyes on me. Females see a nice car or a nice truck and they automatically find a reason to be near you. I just got out, so fuck it.

"Well damn I didn't sleep with you last night Amin."

"Well shit it would've been nice if you did."

As I keep walking to get into the store acting like I'm not pressed she say's something that gets my attention.

"Damn you must've been fucked up at the bar. You don't remember me Amin?"

"Wait a minute don't tell me we did sleep together."

"I'm Sheena. Tina's girlfriend. You remember me now?"

"Oh shit, ok. The quiet one. Ok, I know who you are now. What's good baby?"

"Ain't too much. I seen the truck and it reminded me of you. Then it started looking like you. Do you live around here somewhere?"

"Naw just cruising around sightseeing; checking out pretty girls like you?"

"Like me huh?"

"Yup. You look different up close and personal. You still looking good tho."

"Where you find them Gucci's at nigga? Dem' joints looking good on your feet right now."

"Awe thanks baby. I had these joints on my mind for a nice minute. So was you on your way to this corner store?"

"Shit if you weren't busy, we could go out the park with some drinks and kick it."

"Right then the next minute you fucking the shit out of me. Right?"

"Well not exactly. I didn't get too much rest last night. I was thinking more like you get on top and enjoy yourself a little bit." Sheena gets up close to me and grabs the love muscle then left a comment.

"Umm, ok, But Amin, it's a gun fight about to go down. I don't think it's safe to just stand here. Bullets can start flying at any giving time."

"Well shit, I talk to you later I'm out."

"Hold up nigga! You just gone leave me in the line of fire just like that?"

"Excuse me but what's your name again? Sike come on if you coming."

I think I played this right. I can't act too thirsty when you know they looking good. But damn I didn't even recognize her. I guess it's because of the micro-braids she got in her hair. Damn this girl looks like a dark skinned Toni Braxton with a nice ass on her. She also has the sexiest lips in the world. In my mind she is already giving me head. But if this Tina's girlfriend and she got in my truck anyway then basically she already has plans to fuck me. I'm just not too sure about the suck me part.

66

Life on the Run

"So, Amin, what you and Tina related?"

"Something like that."

"Well did you fuck her before?"

"Nope."

"That nope was suspect."

"No, you suspect, asking me all these damn questions. Is you the police?"

"You funny as shit Amin."

It begins to drizzle so the park just got eliminated off the to-do list.

"Now what Sheena?"

"Amin, you can come chill at the crib if you want. Everybody going in the house now anyway. Or we can pick another day to chill; take my number and we can link up later."

"Damn speaking of a call I have to buy me a phone to make one. Take this ride with me baby."

"How you on top and don't have a phone Amin?"

"Well I just had a fire and lost everything. So you know I'm in get it all back mode right now."

"I can make a small donation if that will make you feel any better."

"So, that's how you want me to feel? A little better?"

"Yup."

"Well let's go to your crib so I can see what them walls feel like. But shit you don't have a famous front door, do you?"

"Famous, you said?"

"Yes, like every five minutes somebody coming or going out your house."

"Oh, no! I live by myself and don't keep a lot of company. I like to keep my business in my life and out of everybody's mouth as much as I could. People would remix you better than a deejay."

I went and got me a Galaxy s 4 and this phone is amazing. Shit, I don't even want no pussy now. But I'm nosey. I like to hear how sexy her moans & screams is and how many different faces I can have her make as I go deeper and deeper.

"You know what I meant to ask you Sheena?"

"What's that Amin?"

"Who ate my damn shrimps I had in the back seat that night? Shit just got real, I knew I was going to catch one of yaw now explain."

"Amin, Saleema was back here fuckin them joints up. Then offered us some while you were halling ass on the highway. I couldn't believe she did that. Her mouth was all greasy when she got out the Truck."

"Sheena I had my mouth ready for them joints. I just knew I had a special in the truck waiting for a nigga. Then here she come, buying me some more. What's her phone number?"

"Ok but you didn't hear it from me. Tell her you watched her eat your shit and didn't say nothing and you felt like she had to be that fuckin hungry, Amin don't throw me under the bus. That's my sister."

CHAPTER SEVEN

Sitting on the sofa watching the First 48, waiting for Sheena to come back down stairs from using the bathroom, here comes a knock at the door. Her sister Saleema politely turns the knob, then invites herself in looking me in my face like she thinks she know me from somewhere. Then yells at the top of her lungs for her sister Sheena.

"Umm excuse me miss, but you do remember me. Right?"

"Amin something like that. Right?"

"You damn right and I'm here so you can take me to get some more shrimps because you left me four shrimps."

"Wait a minute you can't be serious."

"This seem like a fuckin game. Saleema?"

"No. I'm saying like wow, is my sister alright? You didn't kill my sister and was waiting for me to come about these shrimps, was you?" I'm trying with everything in my power not to laugh. But this bitch is crying talking about is her sister alright. She been smoking that shit.

"No baby I'm just joking. It's not that deep. I did want my shrimps. But you needed them more. I was just fuckin with you."

"Why are you here then?"

"I'm here with your sister."

"You fuckin my sister Amin?"

"Not right now. I'm talking to you."

"Can I hold something. I'm fucked up?"

"Hold something like?"

"Anything Amin or do you want me to earn it?"

"What would you do to earn it?"

69

"I'll suck your dick."

"You suck a mean one?"

"Yes, let me show you."

"Ok I let you show me next week because this one is a busy one."

"Come on Amin. Well is it anything else I can do? I need to scrape up five thousand dollars before next month. I will do anything. Just keep me in mind, because you know you want this pussy nigga. I look too good for you to turn me down."

"He don't give a fuck what you look like Saleema get the fuck out my house. I see you would cross any fucking body even me. Bitch leave my house before this shit keeps replaying in my head."

Damn I couldn't hear Sheena coming down the stairs and neither did Saleema but she had to stop before she got all the way downstairs and listened to her sister promoting herself. She scared the hell out of me just now.

"Sheena, you know I don't mean no harm. What the fuck would you do if you had to go through this storm by yourself?"

"For one Saleema, you created your own storm, you knew it was rain coming and refused to invest in an umbrella. So who's fault is it yours or the storm?"

"But damn, this not either one of our man. So why you so overprotective about this nigga?"

"If this nigga in my house Saleema, then evidently it's something good about to happen on my end. You can't fix this one and I guess it's everybody else fault that you lost your man when that was a good man. You knew you didn't have shit. So damn you just don't give a fuck about nobody, not even yourself. But your dumbass forgot you had something good that gave a fuck about you. just get the fuck out my house Saleema!" While the "WHAT

Life on the Run

THE HELL I JUST DO" look is marinating on Saleema's face, we all get distracted by a knock at the door.

"Come on Saleema, chop, chop." As Sheena opens the door I see Tina was the one knocking, coming in looking at me like, fuck you doing here.

"Hey girls I just figured I drop by to say hello and get this nigga mind off some pussy for a minute. He'll be back right after these messages. Come on Amin, let's go."

Damn I feel like my mom just came to pick me up from school or some shit. But it seems as if she knew I was here already for some odd reason.

"Amin, you a hot mess I thought I told you not to fuck with Saleema."

"No, it wasn't Saleema. I was on chills with Sheena."

"Oh, is that right? I wouldn't advise you to deal with her either."

"Why is that Tina let me find out you a hater."

"Oh, never that honey. It's just her, she would make you fall head over heels in love with her and you wouldn't want to do shit else but her. And love can't be loved right now because love will fuck our plans up. It would change how you feel towards what you're up against and that will piss Hassan all the way off.

"Oh, ok you sound right so far."

"Amin I been sounding right ever since you heard my voice now what I did was got you some more shrimps because you was mad as hell. Amin I was tripping off how heated you were. But one thing I'll tell you is, that those are my girls. I call the shots there because they really don't have no direction. They just want to be fly and get high off the compliments they get for their bodies. So basically, what I suggest is you find a woman your personality can handle. Now what we about to do is have a meeting with Hassan.

Amin just to let you know Hassan put a tracking device on your truck and that be the reason why I took your truck this morning."

"So, wait a minute Tina, Hassan has me under a microscope?"

"Yes, he does this is what this meeting is about."

"Wow, so what be his reason why he need to know my every move?"

"I just told you. It's all going to come out in this meeting." Tina puts on her four way flashers as we're pulling up behind a white stretched Mercedes Benz limousine. Hassan gets out the back with the American dream smile on his face as he stares in our direction waving for me & Tina to join him.

"Well here we go Patna." I'm glad I did get cute for today because now I look like supposed to be in this limo. My heart falls in my stomach as I bend down to get in the limo and lay eyes directly on my mother, already sitting in the limo dressed to impress. Fresh hairdo, all white linen suit, with white alligator loafers, with her legs crossed looking like a boss.

"Well hey son, I guess you wasn't prepared to see me right about now. Huh baby?"

"No because I just seen you earlier." Hassan shuts the door and begins to speak.

"Ok looks like everybody's here. Amin I see you clean up pretty well and thank you for not dressing like a thug. You do need a more casual look but this is why we're here today. Okay Amin, are you mentally prepped on what you're about to be doing in the next couple years as Tina explained to you?"

"Yes, I knew it had to be a rough task but at least I'm not in jail."

"That's right and you are aware that by you being an African American with capital murder charges with a Rico Act and no

money for a lawyer that you would've served no less than a life
sentence incarceration. Do you understand me?"

"Yes, I understand?"

"So again, do you confess to return the favor as we discussed while
you were locked up?"

"Yes, I do."

"Ok Pearl can you bring some knowledge about your affiliation to
this meeting."

"Yes. Amin me & Hassan go back like seeds in the flower pots and
the way we grew was fantastic, but what I can tell you is that
you're in good hands like All-state. He got me out some trouble
and I ended up falling back in it. I had to keep the heat to myself
but I gave it a shot by recommending you for the job. Since you
ended up in quick sand, with nobody to get your sucka-for-love ass
out. Now basically you're going to be mixing and mingling with
cartels and Mafia's doing big boy shit. You will have to watch
your ass as if a gay guy was standing behind you with a smile on
his face. You will have to be a cold blooded killer, a murderer if
you had to. Because the last thing you need to happen is for you to
get kidnapped. Trust & believe you will die. Hassan has his folks
over there in Mexico. I really liked it over there too. Hassan my
memories is still going strong. This meeting is about you seeing it
with your own two eyes that me and Hassan know each other. Just
to make you feel a little better about this. Okay baby?"

"Ok mom."

"Now Amin, what I did was put a Tracking device on your truck so
I can monitor the infected parts of the streets that you may not be
aware of. Like where people that's under investigation by the feds,
confidential informants and flat out rats be. It's been a lot that
happened since you were in jail, things changed and you need to
stay solo. So Tina, whatever it takes, keep him happy. You can

start by introducing him to his Mansion and PLEASE go see your probation officer first thing tomorrow."

"Ok I will." Hassan closed it out and before I can get out I seen Hassan pass my mother an envelope. I already know it was loaded with Cash. What the fuck she just sold me or something? Walking back to my truck I'm wondering why Tina left her car down Sheena's. I guess I'm stuck with her again.

"Amin you got it easy nigga. I was scared to death flying with all that shit by myself. This go round the security guards at the airport is on payroll. You still can't sleep on the ones that's not on pay roll. I will show you who's who when we cross that bridge. But this mansion of yours, I'm surprised he gave it to you. He told me while you were in jail he had a house for you in Ridley, PA. But I see when your mom get in shit, things change. I remember this mansion, it's up in Delaware County. This the joint that damn neat burnt to the ground. That fire was all over the news. I guess he got it up and running again and if you fuck any of them bitches, never take them to your safe haven. They would prey on your good side thinking they hit the jackpot. I'm so curious about what this fucka look like now."

CHAPTER EIGHT

I guess we're here at my mansion and what the fuck am I going to do with all this space? The outside is freshly manicured with enough land to handle a Home Depot or a Wal-Mart with ease. The driveway is long, leading up to a small set of historical gates for entering. The historical bricks in the exterior walls seem to be recently power washed. As I enter the mansion, I fall head first in disbelief because it's absolutely beautiful in here, Tina is speechless, and the look on her face is priceless.

The walls are bright white, the ceilings are amazon high, dual curved marble stairs. Damn! This Kitchen will make you want to learn how to cook if you didn't know how to. The stove and sink are combined together that rises from the center of the kitchen floor. The indoor backyard has a romantic decorated Jacuzzi. Now the way this Jacuzzi is decorated tells me that the maid is a woman with all these pretty colorful roses floating in the water. What the fuck is she about to propose to me or something?

"Amin what are you going to do with all this space? You know you have a movie theater downstairs in the basement? Like a real movie theater with the ovens in the back of a glass counter for pizzas & Stromboli's nigga. Shit after seeing this, I might just sign this pussy over nigga. Damn! This motherfucker didn't do none of this shit for me. Your mom put fear in that nigga. I see how she look at him while she's talking to him and how he reacts to what she says. Your mom must be a fuckn' OG triple, triple chick. Because, damn!"

Damn I was hoping the basement was empty because if somebody was to break in for a home invasion the first place they would think of is going upstairs. When I can be downstairs clocking their every move from the cameras in the basement. Oh well, I guess I keep a gun in every room and under every couch. I'm feeling the fears of a rich man already.

"Amin, you have to go bed shopping because none of the bedrooms has beds in it. It's damn near fourteen bedrooms in here and two bathrooms in each one. Like I'm fuckn' loving this place already boy."

Three Hours Later

 Leaving my new mansion feeling like a changed man. Tina is a little different. She's still in deep thought about what we just seen. I wonder if she's over there picturing us on some happily ever after shit, or is she wondering if we even make it out alive from going back and forth overseas drug trafficking to even enjoy this way of living. I guess I have one reward up front.

"So, Tina you want to Decorate it for me?

"Amin that's a whole lot of decorating. Why me? What I look like making it look nice for another bitch to enjoy."

"Wow was that jealousy I just heard? Another bitch?"

I guess something is growing in her for me and she's not discussing it with me yet but I can understand why she rather keep it to herself.

"No Tina, I just can't get anybody. So what you saying, hire a professional?"

"No. I don't know. This might be a difficult task for me Amin."

"What now?"

"No what I get is that, we're going to keep fucking and then you're going to dump me like a piece of shit that just fell from your ass, when you find a chick. Because you know we can't be together.

Amin you felt so good in me. That made me size you up and what I came up with is nothing but good. You're changeable for the good and I read you deep down. I know you're a good man but what's eating me alive is, that I know I can't have you."

"Well that's life Tina. It's always going to be things you want but can't have."

"I see you taking me for a joke too. I shouldn't have ever fucked you. Now I feel like you can have me anyway you want to. Like I'm your puppet or something."

"Well, can I have you anyway I want to?"

"Take me to my car Amin. I don't have time for this shit."

This is taking me by surprise, I didn't underestimate the possibility of her falling for me. I just didn't expect it to happen this fast. Now I might have to hide from her and give some time for my love spell to wear off.

CHAPTER NINE

Tina gave in and decorated almost the whole mansion for me and is now cooking some Alaskan crab legs, muscles, jumbo shrimps with broccoli and corn. Her famous bottle of Grey Goose is on my new king size bed. This bed is making me want to go to sleep. Tina can go somewhere with this purple comforter tho.

One thing a drink can do is turn your fucked-up day into a nice time with only one trip to the liquor Store. Me & Tina is really here trading kid stories; reminiscing off the silly things we did when we were kids. I never laughed so hard in my life. We might need another bottle of this shit.

Smelling dem' Crab Legs is making me want dem' more & more. So shit they need to be up here with us.

Feeling more & more comfortable in my mansion, I begin to walk around with a little more confidence, but that's only when Tina's here or somebody here with me. Because it's so spacious in here till the point it's spooky as hell and it always feel like people are in here with me. Shit let me hear one voice call my name while all the lights out. It will be ass and elbows of me getting the fuck out of here. I haven't even seen all of this place yet either. I just hope it's no animals living here with me.

Coming upstairs with two trays of seafood, I walk in the room to see Tina in a red Victoria Secret set, looking glamourous. But the funny part about it is, she acts as if I'm not in here. It be nice if she keeps up the act while I fuck these crab legs up. Then I act dumb like, oh shit I didn't even know you was in here. Knowing that shit will start an argument.

Life on the Run

"Amin you're the man just like they said you're were."

"You talking about these crab legs or this African table leg?"

"Both, you freak. You only my friend because your ass hungry."

"No I'm actually impressed with your hospitality."

Tina phone rings and suddenly she excuses herself. I believed her when she said that she's single. And that's Hassan. But what the fuck is the secret conversation about? Then again, she might not belong, chilling with me like this, at the same time. But I wonder if Hassan tapping that ass? Hmm makes me wonder sometimes. Tina comes out the room looking exhausted.

"Amin put some clothes on, Hassan is outside. I guess he got a tracking device on me too or this phone one. I don't put shit pass him with his educated ass. This nigga got all kinds of degrees for shit we shy away from because it looks difficult."

When I open my front door, I see Hassan has a brand-new luxury van backed up to my steps with the back doors wide open, with stacks of boxes in my view. But when he sees us.

"Hey Amin how's it going so far, did you ever get a cellphone?"

"Hell yeah."

"Ok, well never call me on that phone. I have a phone for you to talk to me and Tina on. That's it Amin, me & Tina. And by the way, I'm glad to see you two getting along. But in these boxes are semi-automatic hand guns. Spread the hand guns all around downstairs, like places you'll more likely be. Just in case somebody get in here and catch you while you busy. It will always be a gun near you."

"Is it something I need to watch out for Hassan?"

"Maybe, Maybe not. I have enemies and these guys aren't your average street gang bangers. These people are powerful, just like me. So far I been beating them, thinking I'm winning right now. It won't be long before they find out you're on my team. So make sure you keep eyes in the back of your head without being obviously paranoid. Any car that make you feel like you being followed, you test them by making unnecessary lefts and rights. If it confirms that they are following you, go to a Wal-Mart or somewhere where you can figure if they the police or not. If you feel they not the police, then have them follow you to an open area then kill everybody in the car. You just earned your license to kill. Here, take this black card, it has unlimited funds but you will have to return it once you start going overseas."

"Wow Hassan, why I never got a Black Card, he just came on board?"

"You're a shopaholic Tina. You proved that to me with your own money. You will draw attention on yourself and will end up under investigation on how you got the card. Amin has it. So you also have access to whatever you want. You just have to leave Amin with the card."

"I'm jealous Hassan."

"You came too far to become hardheaded Tina. Just go with the flow this our last run baby."

After all the guns are in the house, I automatically fall in deep thought. This package comes with enemies huh? This nigga, boy I tell you.

"Amin, he must like you or something because he gave you a lot. Then I forgot to tell you that this mansion has an underground tunnel that goes way into another city it's a mini train that get up sixty miles per hour. It was a main water line break at one time right before this joint caught on fire and Hassan got paranoid. He wasn't sure if the tunnel was dug deep enough to be unrecognized. He set you up nice Amin."

"Well I didn't see none of this coming Tina. I was paranoid and confused like hell about this favor. I didn't believe none of this shit to keep it funky."

"I know you didn't. I couldn't tell you all that while you were doing your bid in the penitentiary. With your sexy ass. I like you, because you're pretty organized and most organized people know where they're going in life. No matter what's in front of them. Now is that you or did I just describe another motherfucker?"

"You're funny Tina you need to do a stand up somewhere."

CHAPTER TEN

Morning awakes me with welcoming sunlight, gleaming through the blinds and Tina is nowhere in sight. I can smell her downstairs breaking the kitchen in with breakfast. We didn't even have sex last night. I guess this the beginning of us growing closer. Especially, after Hassan seen Tina in a robe after hours and didn't trip. I guess he do like me. Unless he knows exactly what he's doing.

Tina just got my undivided attention when she walks in the room naked pushing a cart with two hot plates full of home fries with green peppers and onions. The buttery cheese eggs, Italian sausages with buttered toast and jelly. Not to mention, the orange juice. She had to slide out and hit the market while I was snoring. I figured she be itching to get to that stove just because it rises from the floor anyway.

"Well thank you baby. When did we get married?"

"I wasn't thinking about you; it was me that was hungry. I just figured you might want some too."

"Whatever Tina."

"What are we doing today Amin?"

"Be careful how you use the word "WE" Tina."

"Oh, what's that my que?"

"No, I'm just joking with you. I'm not sure how you feel about going hood to hood sightseeing?"

"I guess we can do that since it ain't shit else to do besides shopping."

"See there you go. But I'm all for it."

"Well don't forget to grab a Glock."

Damn, one thing I got to admit is, this girl can cook her ass off. These cheese eggs is winning.

ONE HOUR LATER

The hood will never change, I guess. At the same time, it's a place I call home, standing outside the Deli on 29th & Girard it's always a pleasure to hear two crackheads arguing.

"No! No! fuck no Gerald, that's some bullshit. Every time you get paid somebody always robbing your punk ass. They always catching you when you wasn't looking. Get the fuck outta here. I see your eyes wide enough to see what the fuck going on six blocks down motherfucker."

"Bernice you better go somewhere with that bullshit and change dem' nasty ass panties you got on. You so worried about my check until you forgot to wash your stanking ass. You making me hungry over there smelling like a big bag of onions. Bitch you burning my eyes."

"Gerald I know you not talking with them ran down ass Timberlands on. dey' not even trees no more, they twigs now. At least treat yourself. You good for nothing ass motherfucker."

"No bitch, treat them under arms. Bitch it don't matter what you say you still burn my fuckin eyes over there smelling like a cheese steak with all raw onions. You polluting the air about to get a fine for that shit."

"No you just got a fine because now you and them bullshit lies you tell me. Gotta find somebody else to be with."

"Awe you just mad because I smoked my shit all by myself. I do believe it was me working for this money not your fat stanking ass."

"Whatever Gerald. Fuck you and come get your shit before I start a yard sale."

"Ok, OK, OK take this fifty dollars and shut the fuck up."

"See I knew you had money. I guess I just bust you upside your fucking head the next time I need something to save the aggravation huh Gerald?

"Come here give me kiss you know I love you boo boo."

"Amin I'm not feeling this standing on the corner shit. Who is you looking for? You just miss the hood don't you?"

"I do. But rather not live here no more."

"Come on then, let's hit the mall."

"Let's rock."

She don't know the reason why I pulled over. A familiar face got my attention and it's the victim's family that was giving me the I'm going to kill you look while I was in court. He had his blinker on to turn right but when we caught eye contact he keeps straight, driving real slow, so I already know he was in his rearview looking back at me. Now, I'm waiting for him to turn the corner so he can follow me to his last breath. Yup, just like I expected, here he come.

"Aye baby, we might have to put in some work in the next three minutes."

"You want to make up for last night in the truck Amin?"

"No, I think I got a follower and I think it's one of the victim's family that was in court."

"Ok, speed up so I can get out and look at him. So I can make sure it's him before I blow his fucking head off."

"It's three of them and he's on the phone. It's no telling what he's telling them on the other end but hold up Tina."

"Umm excuse me sir but is it a motherfucking problem?"

"I'm afraid so. You're Amin, right?"

"I'm afraid so. You ready to die bitch? Following me, like you need to be with your family motherfucker. Give me them fuckin keys. You funny looking ass nigga."

"He's a problem. You gotta go, plain & simple."

BOOM, BOOM, BOOM, BOOM, BOOM, BOOM, BOOM, BOOM, BOOM, BOOM, BOOM, BOOM, BOOM, BOOM.

Damn, it feels like I'm in a movie. I only seen eyeballs come out people faces on TV. Brains are scattered all over the windows, all because fuck face felt frogerish and leaped into his own casket. And this not Tina's first time killing either I see.

"Amin you'll get a bitch locked the fuck up. Like what the fuck you staring at dead bodies for? They dead. You about a sick motherfucker."

"It's because I didn't kill nobody in a while Tina. Calm down."

"Calm down! You got me fucked up. After that last bullet nigga, it's time to go. We let off damn near fourteen shots nigga and you get stuck thinking about some shit right after you committed murder. Yeah, I'm starting to see why Hassan doing all this shit, you like his main ingredient to his evil way of doing shit. Just get us back so we can watch the news."

I guess, since I'm the last man standing from the situation and made it back out on the streets, they want to kill me. But now, I need to kidnap some of their family members. So I can find the rest of them, then kill them all because I'm not living my life watching my back every fucking day.

"Tina take the wheel, go grab your car, then come back to scoop me. Shit, I have to get this probation officer visit out the way."

"Amin look at your shirt."

I look down on my shirt and noticed that it's blood splatter all over the front. My P.O. would've booked the shit out me.

But damn, this how I'm living the rest of my life out, like I was there, but I wasn't part of Diamonds plan. Shit, I will rock out with my cock out every chance I get if these people on some ole dumb shit.

"Amin, I'm putting your truck in my garage and you just drive my car till tomorrow. Go buy the same truck, same color, and this how you play a mean mind game with the witnesses, if they got the tag number."

"But if anything, wouldn't it fall on Hassan?"

"When they run these tags it comes back to a motherfucker that been dead for over thirty-years. Then when they get hot, he put the correct tags back on."

"Tina this nigga got it all figured out I see."

"No, this nigga is the fuckin devil Amin. It's beneficial dealing with him. But at all times, your life be on the line more than your freedom. He got enemies with the niggas he did business with overseas and they over here too. That's why he making sure you can blast your way out a situation if you was ever in one. But you only been on the streets a couple days and killed four people on some crazy white bullshit." Looking at the time, I see its getting late and my P.O. will be leaving soon and I still have to go home and change up. Shit how did today turn out like this?

ONE HOUR LATER

Damn near out of breath, running down my steps, shirt buttoned up wrong, wrinkled Rock & Republic jeans with untied Prada's. I'm jumping into Tina's Mercedes to get to this P.O. I hate attending unwanted appointments. Turning out of my driveway, I find myself dodging a head on collision with a Jaguar, when this bitch is on the wrong side of the fuckin street. I dodge the accident, look in my rearview and notice that she's now turning into my driveway. Now who the fuck was that?

Stuck in between decisions. Should I U-turn to see who just pulled in my drive way or do I hall ass to my probation officer? Fuck I need to see who at my damn house. I tell my P. O. I left a pot on or something.

Pulling back into my driveway, I notice it's a woman looking at me like I'm at her fuckin house.

When I pull behind her blocking her in she jumps out in a grey suit with a badge on her belt and begins walking towards me.

"Yes, mam can I help you?"

"Umm yes, I'm here to see Amin Gibson please. Wait a minute that's you, am I correct?'

"Yes, that's me and you are?"

"I am your assigned Probation Officer. My name is Ms. Suzan Miguel and you were supposed to meet with me on your first day of release. What happened to that?"

"Oh, I thought I had at least a week to come see you."

Life on the Run

"Well today was your last day to come see me. But before my supervisor forced me to put a bench warrant on you, I figured I come out and see if I can find you. I apologize for scaring you. I just didn't feel like waiting for cars to let me turn. So is that your Mercedes you're driving?"

"No, it's a friend of mines."

"Do you live alone?"

"Yes."

"May I come in and look around?"

"Yes, why not, can I fix you a cup of tea or get you a soda?"

"No, but I will take a cup of coffee cream & sugar please."

"Wow boy this is a lot for somebody that lives alone. Wait a minute, where's your stove?"

"Got to give it a minute it rises from the floor."

"So, are you rich Mr. Gibson?"

"No, I wish I was. Are you?"

"No, I'm going through a bad divorce. My husband set me up so he can take everything. He got cool with one of my co-workers from my last job and had him make it seem as if we were dating and he really shows up in court to lie on me. I think he fell in love with somebody else."

My probation officer puts her head down and I guess she's fighting her tears as she looks flat down on the floor. I pass her a napkin, she accepts it and wipes her tears."

"Oh shit, I forgot you said the stove was coming up from the floor. That's amazing and excuse my French. It just caught me off guard coming up from the center."

"Here's your coffee, hope you like it."

"So you want to show me around upstairs a bit?"

"Yes no problem."

To be smart, the first room I show her is my bedroom. Because she might have a suit on but her figure can't hide. If she didn't have an ass her hips would get my attention anyway. In the face she looks like a Puerto-Rican Foxy Brown, with that good hair smelling like a fresh shower following her every move. The more she looks around, the more she compliments me. The tone of her voice during the compliment is so sexy.

"So I guess this is your bedroom?"

"Yes excuse my bed I was rushing."

"It's ok, I'm not here for inspection but them Victoria Secret panties on the floor is nice. I see you do have company sometimes."

"Yeah, I'm single. So, I take advantage of my options when I can."

"So you don't have a consistent significant other?"

"No my girlfriend passed away."

"Wow! Oh ok, I remember seeing that in your file."

"So what do you do for a living?'

"I'm headed towards car dealership. My family owns many car lots and plan to set me up to run my own car lot."

"Hmm, must be nice."

"I wish I had that kind of back up. My husband just threw me to the curve because I was working all the time. Now I'm like sinking miserably."

"Well, what do you do to keep your mind off what's really going on?"

"I read and I clean until I get tired, but that's regular."

"This is a lot of space you have for just you. If I wasn't your probation officer, I probably ask to rent a room for my office."

"Well nobody has to know. Are you good at keeping secrets Ms. Suzan?"

"Just call me Suzan. Yes, I can keep a secret."

"Oh ok, because I was thinking behind the fact that you're having legal issues you can come here and keep me company and save your money until the storm passes."

"Now you know I can't do that Amin. I think that was so nice of you. What about your optional friend, what would she have to say about this?"

"She wouldn't be in no other position but to understand."

"Automatically, she would think we're fucking because what would be your purpose of having me here? Wow, did you hear my phone ring? I have thirteen missed calls from my husband. Shit, when he calls it's a problem nowadays But sign these papers where you see the x and write your phone number down so I can contact you, I have to go."

"Ok got you."

My probation officer is going through a lot I see but why when she's beautiful and has a nice body? I guess that's just the introduction to get you in her life so you can meet who the bitch really is. The way she cut her eyes at me at some points made me feel like shit can happen. Shit, let me stop before she lock my ass up.

"Ms. Suzan, I hope things get better for you and don't hesitate to call me if you need me, I signed all papers and I guess I'll see you soon."

"Ok thank you Amin. You have a good one, but I can't get out if you don't move that nice Mercedes from in back of me."

That look once again. Shit, I guess she's going to be on my mind tonight.

"Ok."

Watching as she pulls off she probably jumped right in traffic thinking like "Oh this lil nigga rich." While I'm right here like damn, I wonder what she feels like. I wonder how she sound when it's all the way in? And what her facial expressions look like, as I'm getting creative in that pussy. I guess I'll wait for it to fall in my hands because going for it is risky.

Now that I'm alone, sadness creeps into my emotions. I'm missing the shit out of Karen. I know if we both would've made it out that bullshit together, she would be here. I wish the whole team was back but sheesh, who seen all that coming? Now I'm in question about my own identity. Who the fuck did I become?"

The sound of a beeping horn gets my attention. I sneak peek through the blinds and see Tina sitting high in a spanking brand-new black on black Tahoe, like she the police or something. All she need is a long ass antenna on the back of that tented window and she can pull a motherfucker over.

"Don't just look come outside and no hating allowed about my truck nigga."

Shit I wonder where I put the black card.

"Amin something in my bones is telling me you still have that dirty ass gun on you some way somehow. Say it ain't so?"

"It's in the Caddy."

"Did you ever go see your probation officer Amin? You not supposed to be here this early?"

"She came here. Damn near hit me head on."

"Well come on let's get the gun, then grab some lunch in my new truck. I made Hassan feel bad so he told me to treat myself to a truck less than fifty thousand. I got TV's in here. We got to get that gun to our welder so he can melt that joint."

"You all happy. Go sit your happy ass down somewhere and I'm trying to get fucked tonight so what we doing sir?"

Life on the Run

"I'm charging now Tina. This dick was never free. What I gave you was a sample."

"Nigga you tripping. You fucking me tonight."

"Nope, not unless you let me put it in your ass."

"Well you bend your ass over and let me do you first then."

"Tina cut the shit please."

"No you cut the shit Amin. I guess I gotta slobber all over your dick for you to want me. Like what is it about me that's not upgrading your interest for me?"

"Baby your beautiful and sexier than the America's Top Model, but Tina I'm hurt, my feeling is fucked up. I cry at night sometimes. Have you ever loss somebody you just fell in love with? It seems like it really hit me when I got out of jail. I thought the story went like, she's dead and I'm doing life, praying for the death penalty because life in jail is a killer anyway."

"Well thanks for sharing. I so didn't know that was going on inside you. But ok I see where you are but are you coming back any time soon?"

"See you still want to play, but no. When we caught them bodies earlier it gave me a flash back."

"I guess you really don't want me. That was a good one tho."

"You never chillin Tina."

"No, you gon be chilling for real, right back up state road if your ass don't hop out and get that gun nigga."

Hoping back in the truck with this dirty ass gun, reality hits me. I really want out of this life but still I'm happy I'm not in jail. Shit, we all gotta do what we gotta do until we realize what it is we have to do. Oh well, it is what it is.

CHAPTER TWELVE

Suzan found her spot and shit. I should've picked that room but never had time to look around this joint. This joint gets scary at night. I swear I be hearing shit. Suzan has the room that has the front street view, where I can see the river and all the boats and night lights on the bridge. I know she's not leaving no time soon. I'm now hearing a second set of footsteps. Oh boy here we go.

"Hey baby boy." Tina gets stuck when she sees Suzan.

"Tina this is Suzan; Suzan this is Tina."

"Hello Suzan."

"Hello Tina."

"Amin, can I speak with you for a minute please?"

"He will be right back in just a bit."

"Ok."

"Umm who is the pretty girl looking at me like I'm in her spot?"

"That's my probation officer. It's a long story but she will be here with us for a minute."

"Did you say us?"

"Yes I did."

"Well my house is ready. I had to go apply some pressure on the Mexicans working on my shit. My house was supposed to been ready. Damn, but home girl looking good, is we sharing?"

"Oh, shit you bi-sexual Tina?"

"Oh shit, I ain't Bi-polar Amin. Sike. No I'm sometimey with it but that bitch looks good. I might wanna nibble on that pussy. Now don't take me wrong I just wanna nibble."

"Well leave her be before you end up turning her against me."

94

"Yo, this is crazy. This nigga done moved his probation officer in. Your pimp status just went over my motherfuckin head. You winning like shit. I'm about to leave Amin, but can you put in my stomach before I go?"

"That might run you a lil something."

"Stop playing and come on." Tina lifts her fitted mini skirt up and bends over and wow, she's not wearing any panties. I'm turned on instantly as her pretty shaved pussy greets me from the back. Anxiously, I'm going inside her grabbing her by the waist pulling her towards me as her warm walls grip me like they miss me. Since she's leaving I guess I won't cum until she done came damn near five times. Lay my mark in this pussy till further notice.

"Baby you feel so good, you feel so good, awe fuck me…Oooohhh Amin, Amin, Amin, Oooohhh, shit what the fuck, why is you fuckin me like this?"

"Turn around and open your mouth."

I put my dick in her mouth, then grab her by her ponytail and have sex with her face for a few. I want to have a lil fun in here but the sound effects turning me way pass on, I can feel it coming and I know she can too but, but, but Oooohhh shhiittt,

"Damn girl. The fuck."

What just made me sick to my stomach is she just gave me a shy giggle but I don't remember her spitting it out. I guess she calling herself laying her mark but for me it's confirmation that she feeling me. Exactly what I needed because if she loves me then she would die for me if she had to. I definitely need that in my team player. When it comes to going overseas doing dirt because I would most definitely die for her trying to save her. For one, I wouldn't want to be over that bitch by myself.

"Amin, I'm falling in love with you and I hope you not offended because if that's the case why you fuck me like you miss me? I be wanting to lip lock while you getting deep in me but I be hesitant because either you have a guard up or I'm just not your type. Your freak ass still forcing your dick as far as you can get it in me tho. I don't know but, it will all come out and I wish the fuck you would fall in love with this little closet freak listening outside this door. That's why I was loud, (HA HA), I'm out I call you boo."

Damn, now all I need now is a shower and a mean ass chef salad then lay-up watch a movie with Suzan, twinkling my toes, talk some shit to keep her mind off her losses. I guess I have to talk about buying her a house then. Maybe I will meet the real her. I need to test this black card anyway.

CHAPTER ELEVEN

Sitting in the Cheesecake Factory looking at the remains from a big butter steak, baked potatoes with broccoli and cheese, jumbo shrimps with a tall glass of Pepsi, my eyes were most definitely bigger than my stomach. But it smelled so good in here when I walked in. Shit I wanted the whole fucking menu.

"Amin you good over there big homie?"

"I can't move."

"Well you know you don't have to go home but your ass have to get up and let somebody else get this table. It's packed in here Amin."

"You like saying my name don't you?"

"Umm, yes."

"You nasty Tina."

As I'm getting up from the table, I lock eyes on the TV when I see breaking news coming on. I'm so prepared to see our work, but to my surprise, it's just a house fire. Then I suddenly see a face I think I seen before on the news about the fire. Then it hits me. "Oh shit!" That's my probation officer being comforted by firefighters. So that must be her house on fire, and that's probably the reason why her husband was blowing her shit up like that. It looks like she just lost everything.

"So Amin, when are you getting your hot ass truck out my Garage?"

"When it gets dark. Don't stalk me either Tina."

"I'm fucking with you. Stop bitching nigga and buy something else till shit calm down. So far I didn't hear nothing, what about you?"

"I never had my ear to the street. Fuck that nigga."

"Oh, ok. Well finish living and learning nigga. This what's about to happen, I'm about to make a move. Amin get home and open them boxes and find somewhere to put them guns. You didn't even realize they were right in front of your probation officer's face. You are crazy and I know you wasn't expecting her. Pick some hand guns out for us."

"Hell no I didn't know she was coming here. I'm glad it's out the way. Sheesh."

Back at the mansion and my phone starts ringing from a 686 number. This looks like the police calling.

"Hello?"

"Hey Amin, this is your probation officer, Ms. Suzan from earlier?"

"Yes."

"Oh, I'm calling to ask; did you find a lady's purse outside your home? It has everything in there."

"No I didn't see anything. Is everything ok?"

"No it's not. My house just burnt to the ground. If I don't find my purse, I might be fucked for tonight and can't go into work tomorrow. This shit is crazy. I think my husband is behind it all, so we can be separated. But that's ok, I'm sorry to bother you."

"No don't be sorry, it's ok. When you get a chance come back to see me I have a check for you."

"Awe Bless your heart Amin. Will it be enough for me to get a hotel room?"

"Yes. Just come on before it starts pouring down raining. We're looking for a bad storm tonight."

"Ok, I'm on my way now. I thank you so much. Just know that this is well appreciated with full truth Amin."

Life on the Run

Knowing she's on her way sends me straight to the shower. The way she cut her eyes at me, at some points got me ready to jump into my white Armani linen set, that's kinda see through. So she can't miss the dick print. I hope she drinks. That would be a plus for me. Open her up, make her laugh, then give her the confirmation feeling that everything will be ok. I want this one. I can see Tina's face now when she lay eyes on Suzan. It just can't be a cat fight and I can't prep Suzan about Tina because she's not going to stay. But become distant and just my probation officer. While I'm in the mirror wondering if I can scrape up sixty more waves by brushing the fuck out my hair over & over again, I hear a horn beeping. I hope this is her. I open the door and it's her, she had to be close already. I give her the hand motion to come in, from afar, I can see the worry sitting in her eyes. I hope she don't get in here and get all emotional & shit. Fuck it my shoulder up for her to cry on.

"Welcome back have a seat, make yourself at home. Did you eat anything yet?"

"Amin my plans were to get home and get my food out the microwave, put my feet up and relax, replay my day and mind my damn business but evidently it wasn't even all like that."

"Well you're more than welcome to eat whatever from my kitchen. Anything for you to come back to yourself. Oh and before I forget here's that check I said I had for you."

"How much is this Amin? This feels like a bit too much for somebody that just got out of jail. I hope you're not selling drugs."

"Why can't I just be loved? Can't you feel it?"

"Yes I can. But tell me your point in doing all this for me?"

"Oh, that's a story to be told later on down the road, not right now. Anything else mam?"

"No, but I see you have a smart mouth."

"Ms. Suzan, when was the last time you been to Jamaica?"

"Call me Suzan Amin. You are making me feel old."

"Well aren't you like 60-years old Suzan?"

"So I look 60 Amin?"

"Don't tell me your older than that now, shit."

"You got jokes I see. I know you was looking at my ass when I left the last time too."

"To be honest, yes, my eyes were in that area, because I was looking for where your butt could've been, because it goes straight down from your back like you been getting slammed up against the wall from the police all your life."

"Oh my goodness you got jokes. Go apply at the Apollo and do a stand up. Everybody will be laughing at you but not with you. I promise."

Suzan begins to count the money I gave her and I watch as her eyes began to water. I casually walk away to the kitchen as if I didn't see it, to make some coffee. I know at this time she's in troubled waters of survival. So I guess aiming for sex right now would make her feel less than a woman because she probably feels like she has to give in to me because I gave her money. Since what goes around comes around, I guess I'll restore her back to who she normally is. Then let it all happen. Have her fall in love with me instead of making her feel like a trick. I definitely need something good coming back my way after this thug life I'm forced to live.

"Hey Suzan there's a menu for King Pizza if you need to order out. Me personally I have a mushroom pizza steak floating around my mind."

"Thank you Amin, but I'm feeling like I need to book a hotel room before it gets too late, so I can figure out where my next home is. I can't wait till they determine the cause for this fire."

Life on the Run

"Well if you can keep a secret like you said you can, you can stay here until you get yourself back on track and save that petty cash for the small stuff."

"I think I might take you up on that offer. Can I look around to see where I'll feel comfortable?"

"Shop till you drop love."

As Suzan walks away, I notice the new switch she has in her walk. She looks back and I allow her to see me watching.

"Hmm, I must have a nice looking back. Huh Amin?"

"Yes, it's nice and flat."

"I bet if I fucked you, you'll be on probation for the rest of your life."

"Nope, now how much you wanna bet Suzan?"

"Ha, Ha somebody's horny. I can't believe I'm really having this conversation with you. You better know how to keep your mouth shut."

"I'm not a promoter of putting my business out there in the streets anyway, it's ok to relax."

CHAPTER THIRTEEN

Coming out the shower feeling like a Million bucks I guess today is a stay in day, scroll through Facebook & Instagram and trip off people post. I don't know where people get them post from but they be funny as shit.

Drying off singing some Earth Wind & Fire I can hear Suzan calling me. She must be lost. I step outside my door and see her not too far from my room looking around sightseeing. I'm glad I have somebody here with me now.

"Suzan, I been watching you look lost for the last ten minutes is everything ok?"

"Yes, I was looking for you because I ordered that mushroom cheese steak you wanted and it's getting cold. Umm where's Tina at, isn't that her name?"

"Yeah she stepped off, just came to holla. You know how that go."

"Yeah I do. Buss that ass, then send her on her way. I think I like the way you do shit, fresh out the shower smelling like that Kenneth Cole Black & shit."

"Where's that cheese steak baby, I'm hungry?"

 "I'll bring it back with me."

I sometimes wish I can fast forward us just to see what type of woman she is because when a woman is beautiful with a body and still get left, that represents a problem. I can give a shit and a half; but just a little curious at the same time.

"Here you go love, that famous steak that's been on your mind, with some cheese fries and a great Pepsi."

"Wow, what did I do to deserve all this?"

"It's just you, with that big heart of yours, you're my kind of guy Amin."

"Well it's you too, with that love you forever face you have. I like that walk too."

"I guess you scared to tell me how good my ass looks huh?"

"No not at all. You know you got a fat ass, so what, you needed to hear me say it?"

"You funny. So, how long am I welcome in your Castle?"

"It depends on how long you want to stay."

"This sounds so easy. What's the catch Amin, you want to fuck me don't you?"

"No, I'm trying to figure out if you might've needed the comfort of your own home. Which I believe so."

"I do. But getting all that back will take a miracle and some blessings. I lost a lot in this premeditated fire. I know my husband did this."

"Well since you're not through with your divorce, I can buy you a house and keep it in my name until you all done. How that sound?"

"Shit, now it sounds like you want to marry me. What's up with you Amin?"

"Take it or leave it."

"I'll take it."

"Like I thought."

"Boy, if you do this for me I'm yours forever."

"Not so fast you sneaky little thing you. You wanna do the ooochie coochie don't you?"

"No comment. You got some shit with you. The ooochie coochie Amin?"

"No fool, no fun."

"You really lay a good impression on me because baby boy, I would be somewhere in tears right now if you didn't bring me joy and I thank you again. It's very huge in here Amin and it's clean and fresh everywhere. This what helps a lot and all this was right on time. Even though I might lose everything dealing with this clown ass husband of mine, I'm still going to be ok. What hurts me the most is that he's been after my best friend Karima for years. I know my friend. She's coming to court on my behalf with recorded conversations that she let me hear as he was kicking his bullshit game. I never said anything to him because I been undecided about if I should kill his snake ass or if I should just let her fuck him behind the fact she's HIV positive. I'm just trying to let it all sink in right now. So I can know how to balance it out."

"Wow you have quite a story here Suzan. Damn, what can I say besides he brought it on himself. You can't gamble with love because hate is only on the other side of the coin and sometimes unsettled emotional waters will flip the coin."

"I do feel you but how you feel about blowing this nigga brains a block away?"

"Damn a block away?

"Amin, you think I'm playing nigga?"

"Ok, so if his shit just a half a block away then we got issues?"

"Amin, you already got issues, you good, and I like you. I think about you at night when I'm playing with my toy. So, with that being said, I want him dead, so we can be together."

"I never said I wanted to be with you Suzan."

"And your absolutely right. I'm not blind either motherfucker. I see what happens in your eyes when we're staring at each other. I saw that look before and it's an authentic look. Think about the real reason why you passing off checks and taking me in. So umm, if you keep straight, then make a right, and a sharp left; there you will see where you got me fucked up." In a loss for words. The little kid school picture smile appears on my face because she's on to something that was too soon for me to explain to her. The plan was to pull her in but I can also feel her grip pulling me in towards her as well.

"Amin, I should put that dumb ass look you got sitting on your face on Facebook and watch that joint go viral."

"Whatever. My opinion goes like, if he was good to you and it was you that fucked up, then take your loss and learn from it. But if he wasted your time and played with your emotions when you were good to him, then you could either suck it up and charge it to no guarantees in life or you just opt out."

"Your right. But when somebody put you in pain from the manipulation of love, then revenge becomes the option. It's not right, but it turns you evil Amin."

"How about I take you out and show you a nice time. Get a few drinks then go to your favorite restaurant. Then when we get back we get dressed in our birthday suits and show off."

"That sounds great Amin, I really can use a night like that in my life right now. I was in love with this nigga and I guess his feelings derailed from how he felt about me in the beginning."

"Go buy yourself something nice to wear and we go from there."

A ten second stare kept us standing in place as we both noticed the seed of love growing for each other. I hate when that feeling gets in my stomach and makes me feel like I have to go boo-boo. That feeling tells me I'm getting caught up again. One thing I've realized is, that love is contagious and irresistible when it's calling your name.

Suzan done flew out the door and before I can gather my thoughts on what I'm wearing for tonight, I overhear a loud argument arising on the outside of my front door. Now who and why is it so close to my door?

As I open my front door, me and a tall, stocky built Caucasian looking gentleman dressed in all black immediately make eye contact.

"Oh bitch this the nigga you fucking? Is this the nigga you fucking?"

"No I'm not doing anything with him that's my client. Can I do my fucking job and why you so worried Christopher? Isn't that the reason you want a divorce, because you want to be with other people? Don't you fantasize about fucking that bitch Kayla and can't help but to see if it would ever happen? You piece of shit! I looked in her diary and found that she wants you too. So fuck both of you! As of now, you can kiss my ass goodbye or should I kiss you goodbye?"

Her Husband turns to me and starts walking in my direction pointing his finger at me.

"Let me tell you something, I don't know who you are but you better stay the fuck away from my wife and if you seem to have a problem with that I will kill you.

"Sir you have one minute to leave my property. Now you can either leave on your own or I have the coroners escort your dead body chief. Now how we doing this?"

Suzan's Husband looks at the gun I have in my hand then notice the look I have on my face and decides to leave.

"I'm sorry Amin, I so didn't know he was going to come looking for me. He must've went to my job and got my home visitation sheets because I'm always in my rearview just from sending people back to jail. So I don't know. But where did you get the gun?"

"Am I in violation mam?"

"Don't be a smart ass Amin."

"Well just know I have one."

"Amin you might have to watch him now; I know he thinks I'm fucking you."

"Well he's wrong. Especially for giving me more pussy than I was getting."

"Well something has to be done about his dumbass and I'm serious."

Later that night

Fuck it, I guess since I'm about to fuck my probation officer, I can go ahead and roll me a fat joint of that good shit. And since her husband already gave us the credit, I'm going to fuck her so good she's going to want to marry me before she even gets divorced.

"So what you think baby?"

"Oh my goodness!" Suzan comes downstairs with her make up on dressed in a blue fitted dress showing off her diamond necklace and earrings and I never had a foot fetish but the way her feet is done with the matching blue with white designs, is just amazing. how did her husband fuck this one up?

"You're looking amazing Suzan; wow you really is a turn on right now but can I ask you a question?"

"Yes what is it?"

"What kind of drunk are you?

"Fuck kind of question was that Amin?"

"No I just don't want us to get out having a nice time and you get fucked up and start crying & shit. I'm hoping you're not a crying drunk because I will leave your ass crying to somebody you don't even know, on some real shit."

"I wish the fuck you would. How can you be my everything but won't listen to me because I'm emotional?"

"No it's a difference when you drunk. I won't leave you because you frustrating me. I would have to get away from you, behind the fact I would be laughing so hard I wouldn't be able to finish my drink."

"Oh my stars, I see right now I'm going to love you with everything I got because if you're able to turn my sad tears into tears of laughter, then you're the one. I know if you're laughing that damn hard I will start laughing with you and more than likely, I probably won't even know what the fuck I'm laughing at."

"Well you know the rules are accepting the bitter with the sweet in this life we living; so it's nothing more you can do but smile and charge it to nobody's perfect."

"You made my day let's rock out with our cocks out."

"You got one too?"

"Yes motherfucker and its bigger than yours. Now come on dumbass."

I'm feeling myself tonight with my black leather jacket, displaying the black Armani button up laying over top of these throwback black Guess jeans, with some black gators. What makes me look modelish, and I'm killing them tonight with my dark wavy hair.

"Amin, I think I could get you off probation a little sooner. I think I'm going to push for that before I get jammed up and lose my job. If I lost my job how supportive would you be?"

"I'll be in your corner baby. Why you getting paranoid?"

"Because I'm really growing feelings for you and want more of you."

A small portion of affection comes from Suzan's hand as she rubs the back of my head while I'm driving. She's sitting sideways facing me with I'm yours written all over her face. I ducked love with Tina; but this one, I see is going to be a hard one to resist.

Life on the Run

I guess I can enjoy myself tonight with all I been through. I thought my feelings died when Karen clocked out and went home. Obviously, I see it didn't. I find it amazing how things you never thought of really happens in life. But shit, anything is possible I see.

Out the corner of my eye, I observe Suzan as she zones out deep in thought and the seriousness that's sitting on her face exposing more beauty than I give her credit for. I'm feeling so damn weak for this girl and I'm at my greatest to never letting her know. "Amin it's a couple nice spots on South Street and its Friday; I know it'll be live tonight. We can find a spot where it's outdoor seating and camp there for a while, what you think? "Sounds good to me."

Turning off market onto South street I Immediately see life. This is the place to be. when you have the weekend all to yourself. The perfect vacation weather is present providing us with low humidity and a mild 70-degrees, with a peaceful breeze and the aroma of the food is on point. Tonight just might be a good night because I really just found me a parking spot right in front of a restaurant of interest. Me and Suzan are dressed casual so I guess I got to get out and do some casual shit. Like walk around the car and open the door for her, hold her hand, and give her the mafia smile as she's getting out the car in front of these uppity people that's already seated.

"Amin this is a very nice night out and I'm so enjoying your company. I didn't expect my authority to wear off at your front door, due to me being impressed with how your living, but at the end of the day I'm human. I'm not a hoe or somebody that jumps for somebody that's living well. It was the way you scanned me that turned me on. The excitement that was in your eyes told me that I can be me. I felt like I could've fucked you the first time we met."

"So you thought I was easy?"

"No, I seen the lust in your eyes and you have a lot of balls too."

"No, you knew what you were doing before you even came to my mansion with your tight dress pants on, showing off your form. I saw every detail of your pussy; it was showing through your pants. I'm quite sure you made sure it looked exactly like that before coming to my home."

"I think I might want to sit on that honest mouth you got tonight, just to teach you not to speak everything you know Amin. Since you know so much."

As we're opening our menu's the waitress comes with a tray of water but has this confused look on her face, as she looks across the street and when I follow her eyes I notice a big smile on Suzan's husband face as he waves to us.

"Suzan your Husband is here. What the fuck, is he in stalk mode?"

"Stop playing where is he? Oh what the fuck! what is he doing here?"

Christopher is walking over towards us with his phone aimed at me and Suzan. I don't know how to handle this situation because she's legally his wife but let me see how this play out.

"Christopher what are you doing here?"

"Well these are my stomping grounds on Friday's for the bars and spot shopping. It's good to see you're familiar with this part of town; unless this gentlemen showing you around."

"Christopher what do you want, besides a divorce?"

"Bitch I want your soul! You fucking whore."

"I'm not going through this with you right now. Come on baby we're leaving."

"Suzan take the keys I call you in a little bit, me and Christopher have to talk."

"Yes we do."

"Suzan rushes to the car in disappointment while her husband stands overtop of me looking down on me like he ready to bus a move.

"So sir, I see you like my wife. How is she in bed?"

"One thing I have to say is that I'm coming back here to eat so what we can do is walk around the block a couple times and blow some steam off but for the record I guess her sex is amazingly addictive any time it makes you play Joey Greco."

"Listen, me & Suzan have legal issues mixed with a lot of other problems and by her dealing with you, it turns the heat up between us. Now if you want to get burnt in these flames, then be my guest but I suggest you go about your business."

"No, you listen, Suzan is my probation officer. I can't make that decision. She's doing this dinner thing for me to have an up close and personal look at my home plan. Do you have a problem with that sir?"

"I'm afraid so. Because it's more than what it's supposed to be."

"Aye man, what's the gun for? Please don't kill me PLEASE SOMEBODY HELP ME!"

"BOOM, BOOM, BOOM, BOOM, BOOM."

"OHH MY GOD, OH MY GOD! SOMEBODY HELP ME, SOMEBODY HELP ME PLEASE!"

Christopher grabs me as he falls to the ground, leaving a dark blood stain on my jeans. I have to get the fuck out of here. I really didn't give a fuck if he lived or died. You won't threaten me then feel free to pop up talking bout you was in the area. You got me fucked up.

A car is coming up the block behind me and if I turn around and see the police I'm making some noise. A horn blows and to my surprise it's Suzan.

"I guess you had other plans huh? Send me on my way and now I find you walking. When you didn't call me; boy get in here, something told me to swing back through here."

As I'm getting in the car I follow Suzan's eyes directly to the bloodstains on my pants.

"Amin what is that on your pants?"

"I killed your husband."

"Oh my shit! What the fuck! Oh my goodness, boy what made you do that?"

"It's done, fuck why I did it."

"So that means I have three hundred motherfucking thousand dollars coming to a bitch? Boy I knew it was something I liked about you. So what are we going home or what?"

"I have to change up and get rid of these jeans, take the car and get it detailed, I should be ready when you're finished."

"Ok Daddy."

As I'm walking away I'm wondering like Damn I wonder who killed him, me or my ego? I know one thing that motherfucker was serious about killing me about his wife. He could've been a straight scared nigga but when it comes to a nigga love life, oh you better watch your ass.

I jump in a shower and throw on my black & white Adidas sweat suit with some fresh all white shell tops and spray on some Versace cologne to finish my night. Tina got TV's in the Benz so we can watch the news and see what information they got

CHAPTER FOURTEEN

"**A**min, let's hit Penn's Landing and zone out into the river as we knock these bottles off. I got a fifth of Bacardi and a fifth of Peach Amsterdam for the chaser, with some crab legs and clams, all I need is you."

Without too much to say, I'm just analyzing how much happier Suzan became since she learned that I killed her husband. I guess when you get married, it's a lot that's easily tied together, and when you realize the marriage isn't progressing it's a bitch getting things untangled. But what stands out is that love can turn the most caring heart evil.

Sitting by the water rolling a Dutch listening to innocent waters, I exhale as the feeling of peace begins to settle in. My damn cellmate turned me on to this weed thing. It's definitely an escape for now. It also turns me into a freak. I turn straight into porn star. But on some real shit, fuck around be the night she really starts feeling the way she thinks she feels for me. After drinking this liquor, I might get smart and have her rest in peace with her husband and have them talk about what went wrong in their marriage in heaven. Just to make sure she's not that dumb bitch that will accidently throw me under the bus, thinking she has friends she can talk to.

"So now what Amin?"

"Life goes on to breaka, breaka dawn."

"I think you're heartless when it comes to violence Amin and that's not good."

"No, actually I'm a good person. I know the level of anger that rises in men when you sexing their wife, girlfriend, etc. If people actually take their own life behind a relationship slipping through their fingers, what exactly you thought could be on his mind when he came to believe that we could be having sex? All kinds of shit probably ran through his head. He was probably in his head watching me with athletic stamina, hitting you from the back and listening to you scream my name out, telling me you love me. This dude would've blew my socks off."

"Well you have a point there. I didn't think about how I made him feel. I didn't give a fuck how I made him feel. This nigga knew I still loved him. When his side chick goes M. I. A. for a couple of days; this dude would call me and somehow work his way back between my legs. You will do things you would've never thought you'll do; when your heart is not all the way back in your own body Amin."

"I will never understand love. It's nothing a doctor can do for you for emotional pain. That's all love is, nothing but rare pain. You will feel that shit one way or another when you're in love."

"I knew you would understand. So umm how about we take a vacation for a week, let's go to the Bahamas somewhere Amin."

"Shit you late, this liquor and weed got me there already. I'm on a muthafukn surfboard right now; on a big ass wave you got me fucked up once again."

"Shit you sure it's not PCP you smoked?"

"No I said surfboard Sue, that shit you talking about make a nigga feel like he can fly. I know damn well I don't have no wings so umm naw baby no ooowee."

"Oh, ok that just might be some good shit you smoking."

Life on the Run

The more intoxicated I got the more interested I became in having sex with Suzan tonight. I know she down for it but then it's like, Bitch didn't your husband just get murdered? I think I need to be alone for a while, get fucked up, and let the bass from some Pac shit vibrate my chest for a few. Let a nigga zone out without her wanting to talk about her life; distracting me from figuring out where I need to be in my own. Ok, I got a plan. I will set my ringer to vibrate and I will make it seem like it's my nigga. Before I get the chance to activate my plan my phone rings and its Hassan.

"Hello."

"Hey Amin, where are you?"

"I'm in the city."

"Cut the shit Amin where are you?"

"I'm down Penn's Landing by the water."

"I already know where you are; I was just doing a loyalty check."

"Well where are you if you know where I am?"

"I'm behind you."

My Stomach begins to twist as I turn around just to see Hassan really walking up behind me; this just made me uncomfortable.

"Well guess who just happened to be in the neighborhood. Hey how the hell are you?"

"Tell the bitch you will see her some other time. Matter fact, excuse me for a second."

Hassan checks his surroundings, then walks over towards Suzan. My heart slowly falls into my stomach as he pulls his gun out and shoots Suzan in the back of her head. I'm caught off guard. Shocked, I walks off without turning around, but before I can make it to the car, my phone rings and its Hassan.

"Hello?"

"Amin leave the car where it is, you're beginning to be a straight fuck up. I'm pulling up behind you, get in the car."

This is one sneaky muthafucka.

"Now where do I start. Let me see, I guess I'll start from homicide detectives are on a hunt to find the wife of a recently murdered husband and just so happened you two are together here by the water. Now, I didn't wanna ever let this particular cat out the bag, but I see its some shit you just have to be aware of. It's no time that you're not being followed or watched. I have men that take shifts to watch you but its only to make sure that you won't try to fuck me by leaving the state. The shit you get into is making my boys earn their pay because what the FUCK Amin, what are you doing here? They want her ass so bad, till they put her on the news, wanted for questioning. I don't mean to alarm you or to make you feel stalked but protecting my plan includes protecting you. Just to make sure a favor gets returned, one thing I have to tell you is that, there's a chance they might come for you. The only good thing is that you weren't there long enough for anybody to remember exactly who they might be looking for because its busy on South Street. I pulled her up and she definitely had a motive to kill him because he filed for divorce and without him she had nothing, I feel like after hours of interrogation she would've broke down and threw you under the bus."

"So, I assume you have a listening device as well?"

"Well, Tina never had it uninstalled a couple years ago. She used to seduce my partners into telling her how they really feel about me. I couldn't believe half of the shit I heard them say about me. When you have a team that's getting a mass amount of cash and you're the ring leader, you have to monitor your people and their greed. When I feel something in my stomach about somebody; I watch them closely without them even realizing it. I always end up being right. Tina been my girl when it came down to shit like that because they all wanted Tina. She used to act like she couldn't stand me when she would have them in the car. They all wanted her; so getting them into a conversation about how they related to her hate about me, was a piece of cake. Being honest, I didn't mean to snoop in on you, but I'm glad I did. Now about the overseas thing, that's canceled, because if you kill somebody over there, I would probably never see you again. So Mexico and L.A will be our target and three trips max and we're done because I just might need you in a different department in this organization Amin. For now, you're a risk to your own life and freedom. So we're going to rap this transaction process up as soon as possible. Go get some sleep and I will keep my antennas up about this situation, until it passes by. Now get some sleep and be careful who you deal with Amin."

"Ok I got you but what about the car?
I'm outta here."

"Ok later."

Damn the feeling of being in some shit I can't get out of is right back in my damn stomach. I'm hoping that my mom comes with that cold ass bucket of water to wake me up out of this dream. Shit I wish it was. All this got people following me and he listening to me got me mad as shit because what the fuck!

My phone rings from an unrecognized number. Now who can this be?

"Hello?"

"Hey baby, what are you doing?"

"Just got in the crib, where you been at?"

"Amin, I had to get away from you for a minute. To be honest, I was pissed you had moved a bitch in with you. I didn't make too much noise about it and I know we was just fuckin but it's just something in you that I feel is just for me I know it is."

117

"Did you talk to Hassan Tina?"

"You already know I did and you owe me a car chump."

"Why you say that?"

"Because It's gone."

"Shit well I guess I do."

"Amin, I want to move in with you. I was trying to pump myself up to ask but before I had the chance to ask your probation officer moved in. I gotta give it to you, you're a bad muthafucka. This nigga fucked his P. O,, like wow, shit please tell me you home."

"Yeah, I'm home."

"Ok, well I'm pulling up."

"Ok."

Life on the Run

CHAPTER FIFTEEN

"**A**min, you have some mail from the courts baby."

"Awe shit, what the fuck they want now?"

"Open it and find out."

As I opened my mail my eyes begin to water, Suzan kept her word, I'm officially off probation with no need to report back to the courts for nothing.

"So, what it says Amin, you look lost?"

"Suzan took me off probation."

"Wow and she's dead that's crazy. She could've been your downfall. Hassan was mad as hell at you because he felt like the feds was using her to get close to what you do."

"Wait a minute he actually told you all that?"

"This is a mafia your affiliated with Amin this not your average thug life. No matter what, never tell him I told you that. He didn't tell you because you're temporary. There's no need for you to know all that shit. His name fuck around not even be Hassan far as I know."

"He cancelled the overseas mission Tina."

"Oh, shit, did he?"

"Yeah, he don't trust me. He thinks I will have us stuck in jail over there."

"Well shit I'm glad he don't trust you then. So now what?"

"He told me Mexico and L.A. and just a couple trips."

"Oh, now he wants you out his hair I see. That's damn near a hundred thousand dollars for each trip. Then he gave you the black card so how about we do the trips and just leave this life alone because I don't want to live like this no more Amin."

"Me either so after these trips we're through huh?"

"Yeah we can invest into something positive with the money Amin."

"Your right but are you hiding something from me Tina?"

"Hiding what Amin?"

"Are you French?"

"No Weirdo, do I look French?"

"No, I just noticed you say things like, we a lot."

"Oh, you got jokes I see."

"So, I look funny to you Tina?"

"Amin, can you stop; I have a couple questions for you too."

"Oh, boy here we go, is direct eye contact required in this questionnaire?"

"I'm afraid so, now look at me."

"Yes ma'am."

"What exactly happened with your last girlfriend?"

"Wow you really gave me an invitation to a sensitive conversation here Tina."

"I asked you to look at me when you talking to me. Why you avoid eye contact with me Amin?"

"Well, I think it's because I'm really attracted to you, the way you carry yourself, and your ways reminds me so much of my last girlfriend till the point it's scary."

"Did you ever tell me her name?"

"I'm not sure."

"Well what was her name?"

"Karen."

"Did you love her?"

"Yes, I did. I just fell in love with her and this shit happens."

"Won't you tell me about her."

Life on the Run

"Well things took off pretty quick with us. I accidently skipped a day of school on purpose one day with my classmate and we went over his girl crib and Karen was there with his girl so we conversated for a few and I guess the realness of the conversation shifted us on to another level on some real quick shit."

"How did she make you feel about her in that short period?"

"Well from me knowing she understood me that was the beginning of me looking at her as somebody I can talk to. Then she was beautifully intimidating, I stayed original. Her Aroma from her shower made her smell fresh and clean. My mind fell straight in the gutter and evidently hers did too. One thing led to another and wow I was in love. Not to sound like a sucker for love but while I was having sex with her I can tell that pussy wasn't consistently in use. But wait a minute can you handle the conversation you digging in Tina?"

"I'm enjoying it, keep going."

"Ok, she was tight and wet as hell and enjoyed every stroke. I held back so I wouldn't buss so fast, just to make her remember that shit. Her face would wrinkle up in a way a female would be ashamed of and I enjoy that. From that point, I knew I had opened her up wider than I expected and I was open as well. The feelings in my stomach felt like I was in a canoe with no paddles, in the middle of the ocean, headed for the water fall. It's that feeling of knowing you're falling in love and can't do shit to stop it and scared that you'll get hurt when you finally hit the bottom. You feel me?"

"Wow Amin, she sounds like somebody that really had your attention and got it quick too."

"Yeah, she did. You know we come across them special ones that just sweep you right off your feet like slipping on black ice."

"Yeah, I know that feeling. Amin it seems as if you have more angels around you than demons. I think you should side with the angels and never look back after this mission, you hear me?"

"Yes, but damn, you sound like my woman."

"Let me tell you something, if I was your woman you would be the happiest man on the male list. The love I give is fair and authentic and that comes from when I choose. I choose wisely, other words, I already done found that man capable of handling a strong woman, that lives up to the responsibilities of her position; not saying I'm the greatest at making men happy, but when the time comes for me to put my foot down, I make sure my foot is looking good and pretty. You hear me Amin?"

"Loud and clear, I did."

"So, Amin if you came across a woman that gave you integrity, would she be someone you would consider to be your wife?"

"I believe so because you can't fake integrity. It's one too many things to be real about at one time. So my answer is yes."

"To find a woman that can delete your insecurities, how would you propose to her?"

"Well I would probably check in with her father and if everything pans out from there, I would set up a special cruise for him to take her on. She would probably want me to come. I would have so much to do and tell her she should take advantage of the getaway to clear her head. I would be on that same cruise in the back of the kitchen with the chefs waiting for her to order some food and whatever she orders, I would have them show true talent on the presentation of her food. I would be dressed just like a server and when I'd deliver her food. The diamond ring would be sitting on top of her dessert and when she says yes, the music comes on and we start getting it."

"Well ok, that's all I needed from this session. Thanks for your cooperation Amin."

"What? What the fuck was that some kind of interview or something?"

"No just sizing your sense of humor up. You ready for L.A?"

"Let's get it."

"Ok, I will let Hassan know we ready."

Two Weeks Later

When I open my eyes on this fantastic Friday morning my surroundings seem to be peaceful, my window is slightly cracked and the smell of fresh cut grass has made its way around my room. The birds are out chirping and the sunshine is creating Kodak moments all over the city. The only thing that ruins it for me enjoying this nice day, is the fact that today me and Tina will be on the 12:00 flight to California. Let the games begin.

"Oh, so you finally awake huh?"

"Yeah, I'm up baby."

Let's start getting ready. Umm can I sit on your face before we leave? Sike I'm joking. But I do want you before we catch our flight."

"Buss a Move Tina."

Damn, I guess what's meant to happen shall be done. I really let my guards down and agreed to an understanding with Tina. It wasn't that I didn't like her, she just reminds me of Karen so much, to the point, I wish she was her. The fact that she's not, it's like me finding a stack of fake one hundred dollar bills, but behind the fact she wants to do the right thing. I guess my best decision is to give it a try just to help me, help myself from getting killed.

"Amin, you probably don't have an appetite but I advise you to eat something before you get on that plane."

"You said you was going to sit on my face, right?"

"I was joking but serious at the same time and how that sound, but shit I'm nervous and trying to shake it off. One thing about California, gang members are all over there, you have to watch

124

how you hold eye contact with them because they probably get nervous and try to kill you thinking you one of their enemies. To water that down from happening, we're going to dress casual on their asses. So whip out them Gucci loafers and grab some linen and let's go."

Everything she said made sense, all the way to the part where she said, "Let's go" that let's go part just gave me gas. I feel like I better go to the bathroom before I leave.

"Amin Come here."

"Can I help you, ma'am?"

"Yes, I need you to put your dick in my mouth.

"Oh wow! Ok, get all what you need baby."

Instantly I get aroused because Tina is wearing her clear lip gloss today. This the shit that turn a nigga into a minute man early.

"What are you waiting for Amin?"

Tina comes and take charge, pulling my boxers down to my ankles putting the whole situation in her mouth. The sound that it tastes good to her just made me feel like I just came from the gym good and energized. I thought she was just talking shit.

"OH! Damn girl!"

The freak done came out of Tina. The sight of them shiny lips on this dick and the way she keeps looking up at me with them pretty eyes just did it.

"Awwweee, sshhiitttt, damn girl! SHEESH"

"I figured I'd have you release some stress and tension, hoping you fall asleep on the plane. I got some Xanax too. But only dump two because these blues not your twist. It's just no telling how peaceful this flight is gonna be. Hold on this Hassan calling me."

"Hello. Umm hmm."

"Yes, he's right here."

"Ok"

"Amin, here Hassan want you."

"Hey Hassan, what's good?"

"Amin I tried to call you but I couldn't reach you. Listen I need you and Tina to dress down. Don't go over there looking like money, you'll attract the wrong attention and that's the last thing we need right now. You and Tina will be over there for one week, just so you won't have the actions of a trafficker because they monitor shit with all that running back and forth shit. Relax your eyes, don't be looking nervous when you coming back; my boy Hundo will make sure my work gets back to Philadelphia. Just listen to him, the patrol guards are already on point. You just have to leave when I say leave, we clear?"

"Clear"

"Ok. Don't call me when you get over there, I will see you when you two get back have a safe trip."

"Ok"

"Shit, Tina I don't have no cheap clothes and he wants us to dress down."

"Well we have to go, let's rock."

"Well you never told me who's meeting us."

"Oh my bad, I was so in to you it didn't even cross my mind to have that conversation with you. There will be two women dressed as doctor's waiting on us. They will take us to Hondo, then we make the transaction. These nurses will be rolling you back in a wheel chair and everything we need will be in the wheel chair, in your seat, all around the wheels and compressed down in an oxygen tank. Two or three of these trips and your favor is returned and we'll be rich because Hassan is going to let you keep the black card anyway to make sure you keep your mouth shut about our affiliation with him. So put your game face on and focus."

"Bet."

I can't help but to sit back and wonder where is that day that I will be free of crime. I didn't see this lifestyle in my future, but it seems as if it's a package deal that comes with every decision I make. If I learned negative first, then I wonder what's in store for me if I did things the right way. Anybody can pull the trigger, but not everyone has a universal way of thinking. Tina asked me about how would I propose to my woman of interest, I wonder what's her true intentions, and why she so hesitant? I think Tina might wanna take this to another level with me. But at the same time I have to play like she not a factor while showing interest. This shit crazy. You can't show your whole hand because once they know you, you no different than a book they read already, if I didn't learn anything from interactions alone, is that you have to stay interesting and surprising. That's the reason why kids love their parents so much because their parent can't tell the kids everything so they just make shit happen.

Los Angeles California

"Amin, we're here love. You ready to get through this mission?"

"Yeah, I am but the only thing scared me the most, is that we gotta do this without being strapped."

"We'll be ok. Hassan would've made that happen for us if you would've never made him feel like you trigger happy nigga. Calm your black ass down somewhere before you find your ass stuck back in the twist, dumb-dumb."

"After this, I'm doing something different because in this game, it's too easy to get in a situation where you might have to kill something. Greed is like HIV to these streets. Especially, when you don't know when to cash in."

"Well it sounds like you should listen to me when I get to speaking all the right shit then."

"You swear we in a relationship, don't you Tina?"

"Well we be in a relationship when your dick in my mouth don't we? You be in love too, pussy making all them noises. I be like, I wish he shut the fuck up. Now what chump? Why you don't be brushing me off; since you talking shit, we both know you just scared to fall in love Amin."

"No, I'm just scared to fall in love with your crazy ass. Look how you just went World-Star on me."

"Just get your ass off this Plane." brought a nice pair of shades, the ones that's trained for the movement of the eyes. People don't even know you but can tell when you're not yourself and right now, I don't know who the hell I am.

"There go Hondo and them doctors waiting for us Amin. Now, they might flirt with your handsome ass but we don't know these people and what their strategies stand for so focus. The games have just begun."

Looking around observing the scenery, I must admit that this is a pretty environment, the smell of fresh grass and the scenery of these tall palm trees is making me fall in love with L.A. Everything that looks good but I know it has something ugly about it. Probably more than we imagined.

THREE HOURS LATER
THE LUX TOWER HOTEL

I see Hassan is affiliated with some real big boys here in L.A. The women dressed up as doctors, guide us to a luxury room in the basement that has a secret door on the inside of a walk-in closet. Behind the door is a finished tunnel that has a cart that looks like something from Great Adventures. It rides on two tracks like a train. The doctors gave us a ride and I can't believe how fast this little cart is going. I'm feeling at least thirty miles per hour. The ride is about twenty-minutes long underground. When we get to where we needed to be, I was shocked at what I seen, kilos of coke and heroin stacked up on pallets as if they were distributing pampers. The only thing that's not sitting too well with me is that these Columbians are giving us all the evil eye; including the fake doctors. Clearly something is wrong and it seems as if they're not too excited about doing any business with us. Now here comes three Arabian men walking towards us, signaling the driver to move from behind the wheel of the cart. Hondo got out the cart and stood with the doctors. when we get back in the cart, three loud gun shots go off. When I turn around, I see that the women dressed up as doctors along with Hondo has been shot dead. My heart is thumping hard now. But I can't be trusted with a gun, this fuckin Hassan guy. These Arabians that's supposed to be taking us back don't even speak English so what the fuck is about to happen to us. Me and Tina look at each other with fear in our eyes when we notice these motherfuckers isn't taking us back the way we came. I zoom in on their waistlines and I see both of them are carrying guns and the only thing left to do is snatch the guns and turn this situation back on them. But before I can activate my move Tina beat me to it by just snatching the drivers .380.

"STOP THIS CART BEFORE I BLOW YOUR FUCKING HEAD OFF."

"Amin take his gun." I grabbed the partners gun and now we safe again. Unexpectedly Tina let the driver have it. BOOM, BOOM, BOOM.

Before I can get a full grip on the partner's gun, Tina done killed both of them.

"Amin toss his big dumb ass off the cart so we can get the fuck out of here."

Tina finds the reverse on the cart to get us back on the tracks, headed back to the hotel.

"Oh, shit Amin! I don't know where the brake is and this fucker is picking up speed all by itself."

We make it back to the Hotel secret door to find that its locked.

"Amin kick this door in, and you know we on Hassan shit list, now right?"

"Fuck Hassan Tina, he sent us out here with no protection and look what happen."

"The door is down now, let's get the fuck out of here."

"Amin, I have something to tell you baby, since we on the devil's shit list."

"And what is that Tina?"

"It wasn't a coincidence that I got your attention while you were in the twist if you didn't know."

"Ok, now what do you have to tell me Tina?"

"Ok well let me start by saying I knew who you were before you came to jail. I arranged it for you to be where I can be in your presence. I took a leave of absence when you got out so I can spend time with you to see if there was something in you that would make my dream come true."

"And what is your dream Tina, come on tell me"

"Ok that girl Karen, you jumped off the roof with, you remember her?"

"Yes, I do. Why you mention her?"

"That girl Karen was my sister Amin. She was pregnant with a little girl. I had to get close to you because I didn't want you to find out you had a daughter and disappear with my niece. So, I figured I'd ease up on you and lock that ass down and we be a family, so my sister can really be in peace knowing you and Miracle are good on the strength of me. That's why I financially blessed you the way I did."

"Whoa baby wait a minute, run that by me again."

"Yes baby, I was the good sister, Karen was the wild one, like to fight and cuff them big timers on the street. Your mother allowed me to name your daughter but your mother has custody of her. She couldn't tell you about it because she needed you to get that tab straight with Hassan. Now we have to kill him because he's a mess when he's mad Amin. I named her Miracle because she cheated death. I don't think Karen knew she was pregnant. She was six months pregnant but your daughter is healthy and beautiful Amin."

"Wow Tina, you just fucked my head up. I did tell you that you remind me of her."

"And when you would say that it used to touch me because I wanted to tell you so bad, but what I also want to tell is we really need to get out L.A. and put a hit on Hassan because it's us or him now. I think I should at least wait to see how he sound then go from there."

132

"Smart but risky, but ok tell me this Tina, what do you want from me?"

"I want a family from you on the strength of my sister, then I like you at the same time, you definitely not going to have another bitch helping you raise my niece chump that's all I have left from my sister."

"Well I still got my mom Tina."

"Oh, and damn Amin I have some bad news about your mom."

"What the fuck is now Tina?"

"Your mother has stage four Cancer; she didn't want you to know but I'm telling you everything just in case I get killed before you. If we come out of this without getting killed or having to kill somebody, then you definitely have to change your ways because we are all Miracle has you hear me Amin?"

I'm fighting my tears as I stay silent until I know when I do talk, I won't have that shaky voice like I'm about to break down.

"Yes, loud and clear. I want to see her."

"You more than likely walked right pass her when you were down your mom house Amin. That was one of the main reasons your mom was up at the hospital. They did a DNA test on your mom first, then they did one on you to be sure that Miracle was yours."

"Well damn Tina, how did it all come together?"

"Well I met Diamond's mother at the preliminary hearing and Ms. Angel told me everything, but when your mom told me that the doctors delivered a premature baby from my sister, that's when I became extra curious about you. Our family is not supportive. I know Karen would've cherished this little girl. I moved away from my mom and my sister a long time ago, because mom dukes was sticking me for my papers, on some sneaky shit, thinking I wouldn't miss nothing because she was pinching off of racks I had in my bootleg ass stash. Yeah, it made me come to grips to organizing your location so It would be easy getting next to you and now that I did, I don't want to move from your side. So yes Amin, this is more than a coincidental connection with us."

"Wow, I'm so taken by surprise right now. I hope I don't start having personal conversations with myself in public when I get old because this enough to throw a nigga off Tina."

"Well when we get back in Philly, we're getting dressed to kill, because if Hassan feel some type of way about the situation, he has to go ASAP. This man has too much power Amin, you hear me?"

"I heard."

A moment of silence comes in between us as we're boarding our flight and to my surprise, me and Tina gets researched by the guards, as if they missed something in front of everybody on the plane. Shit! Now I'm a little embarrassed. I'm so glad we're not dirty.

"SHEESH!" Hassan didn't have his loyalty down to the oils like he thought, but he did give us a certain time frame to come back too.

PHILADELPHIA

"It's Showtime Amin. And please keep your eyes on everything."

When me and Tina arrive back at the mansion, I notice there's two women casually dressed standing out front of my mansion.

"Amin, you do pop ups?"

"Hell no! Nobody knows where I live. Who the fuck is them?"

When the women notice they have company, they stare at us, patiently waiting for us to get closer and the closer I get the more I see that it's Hassan and whoever this is he has with him dressed as woman. I guess we're about to die right here.

"Hey guys, I'm quite sure you have a hint on why I'm here am I correct?"

"Yes."

"Well Tina, since you so sure, share a little bit with me about what the fuck happened over there.'

"Well it seemed that everything was going according to plan. The ladies took us to the lab, then the next thing you know, we're getting the evil eyes, then they killed the women."

"Wait a minute, did you say they took you to the lab like, to the warehouse?"

"Yes, Hassan they took us through the secret door in the hotel where we got on this roller coaster looking type of cart, then drove us underground to where we needed to be. I didn't know that bullshit was going to happen, so now what? Did that bullshit just cost us our lives?"

"No, but I'm glad I took my main man Kaylo's advice. He told me I should hear you out before I kill you. What you just told me cleared the air because all this happened because the women weren't supposed to take you to the warehouse, they were supposed to put you two in the bathroom to burn enough time for them to come back from the warehouse, then come back and let you two out, it wasn't meant for you to find out anything about nothing on how they do shit. So that's why they killed the girls and best believe you two were next. The only problem I'm having now, is that they still have my money but now they're asking for an additional sixteen million for the deaths of his hit men. I disagreed, then a couple hours later, I get a phone call stating that they're going to kill my whole family off one by one until I pay up. I didn't like the threat. So, I went home to change cars and I had a delivery waiting for me on my steps. I thought it was a bomb in the box so I paid a crackhead five dollars to open it up. When the crackhead opened the box he instantly vomited. I get up on the box, just to see the head of my oldest brother, these cowards put an instant hit out on my family. That's why we're dressed like this. So, you should already know they want you two dead regardless. This mission is cancelled till further notice. I'm going to war. Keep the black card Amin but make sure I'm good if I get locked up. But If I die in this war, the card will be cancelled, so buy some property and play monopoly. Now, you may take me to the guns." As I begin to take my key out to open my door, I can hear Hassan cocking his gun back. "Am I dying after he get these guns or am I just paranoid?"

"Amin, I need you & Tina to keep a low profile, no fancy dressing until I swallow this war. I'm like a president when it comes to this type of war. I have Armies to fight for me just as well as them, but be careful and Amin pay full attention to body language of anybody that gets close to you, we clear? I can't afford to lose you, your loyalty got you in a good place in my heart young fella. You didn't hide these guns too good either, but I will catch up with you soon."

"Ok and I thank you for everything Hassan, your words will recycle in my head."

"You sound smart just don't let a piece of ass turn you into a dead man because that's how they set traps when you become hard to kill."

"Ok that's noted Hassan."

"Peace out."

"Peace."

Watching Hassan as he left my mansion, has been the best thing I've seen since watching the way Karen face wrinkled up as I got deep in her. His words are still here; and my thoughts about Tina and the mind-blowing shit she told me now has space to settle into my mind. I guess Hassan has officially left the building because here's Tina walking in with the thank you Jesus look on her face."

"Amin I'm done, I'm fucking done with this dude and you're done too, and if he comes out on top from this war, then we will kill him ourselves are we clear?"

"Yes, we are. I guess we'll have to take him out in broad day light because I don't feel too good about a set up when it comes to him he's a little advanced."

"So… umm…where we go from here Amin?"

"Shit, let's hit the clock bar on Broad & Erie, I need some seafood."

"No nigga I'm talking about us."

"Well bus a move Tina, if that's how you feel, bus a muthafuckin move."

"Let's hit Macy's and see what they have in there. I just might want to get cute, then get tore up from the floor up, then get back here and go for a joy ride on your face. How that sound Amin?"

"That sounds nasty you freak."

"Well it wasn't nasty when I had all that dick in my mouth, now was it?"

"It damn sure wasn't?"

"Yes, I just had to make sure you were only playing nigga. Since we got that straight, you know we have to get down there to see your mom and Miracle. Amin, it was really killing me inside not to tell you all this, but Hassan and your mom found a special need for you not to know at the moment. He felt like you knowing all of that would've made you back out on him."

Damn with this being Karen sister, with the rehearsal of what all she said replaying in my head, I think I might go ahead and pull her in my heart and lock the doors behind her. She wants to sit on my face and I bet she'll never forget this performance I got waiting on her. Drive that ass straight up the wall.

"Come on baby you ready?"

"Where are we going first Tina?"

"To your mom crib. Do you have a gun on you?"

"No, but fuck that Glock, I'm about to grab one of these Mack-10's I'm ready to split a mufucka in half as soon as they come for me."

"Can you handle that type of fire power? Like on some real shit Amin?"

"Shit, it's no different than operating a chainsaw, just a wireless way of chopping shit down."

"Ok, well we out."

Life on the Run

It feels so good to be back home in these Philly streets; I can't say what I exactly miss but it just feels good to be back home.

TWO HOURS LATER

Pulling off the lot with a brand spanking new, smoked out, limited edition Tahoe. I got me in my big boy bag and Tina is amazed by the sound of the dual exhaust pipes on her smoked-out Marauder, since incognito is the smartest way to move around for a minute. Tina thinks I'm bullshitting about me needing to sit down in the clock bar.

"A baby, you do know I was serious about my seafood, right?"

"Be all you can be Amin, but let's get to your mom's crib first."

"Ok, well we out then."

This joint has satellite radio, playing one of Jay-Z Joints (Some People Hate) this was my shit.

Sitting at the light at 29th and Jefferson Street, looking at some original gangstas just shaking my head because local gangstas be the ones that has that, keep your finger on the trigger beef. All because the enemy knows where to find them. And behind that very reason, these niggas be waiting for a nigga's body language to say the wrong thing, so they can blow a nigga soul out his body As I'm parking in front of my mother's house, this pretty little girl gets my attention. As she just stares out the window I get out and get a better look at the little girl. My emotions attacked me without warning. I can't even knock on the door yet because I'm at my best to not let nobody see or hear me cry. I can't even control it because I already know who this little girl is, it's my daughter, looking just like me & her mother. Before I can collect myself, my daughter disappears from the window, then the door opens and the little girl looks at me. I pick her up and hold her tight as the tears and cries hit me again. I can feel the grip Miracle has around my neck. She knows who I am without asking me. These tears told her. I lift my head and see my mother standing in the middle of her stairs holding her hand around her mouth as tears drips down to the floor from off her hands. I follow my mother's eyes as they went around me. I turn to see what she sees and there's Tina in back of me, sneak crying, avoiding eye contact with me as she looks to the floor, but her embarrassment from her tears just stole my heart.

"Yes, Amin that's your little girl. I really needed to see them tears because I didn't know who you became when the streets got you. Your tears just told me your still my baby. I see you have a good heart, so with that being said, I know you will love this pretty little thing here. Tina lock him down for me, turn him into a man then a husband because those tears he just shed told me he would love you too. Amin, if it's something in her that really wants to complete my wishes, I'd rather you marry this woman. Do you hear me?"

"Yes mom."

"Ok good. Miracle will be here with me until you find a comfort zone for her. With that being said, I'm going to lay down, I'm not feeling too good."

"Ok mom. Love you."

"Love you too, son."

My daughter is feeling around my head with both hands looking into my eyes examining my face. This feeling just did something to me, something that's making me think twice about putting my life and freedom on the line. I think I just want to be here for my baby after seeing her face to face.

"Ok Ms. Pearl, we about to hit Macy's to see what they got in there. We were going shopping for just us, now it's for Miracle too, I see."

"Well save your money because she's a good girl and she's growing fast."

"Well we're not going to hold you no longer Ms. Pearl, you get your rest and we'll be back soon."

"Ok."

As we're leaving, I see Miracle clocks every move I make and I guess my mom don't want me to know about her situation because she would've told me. Tina was probably hoping I didn't bring it up.

"Ok Amin, where are we going?"

"Well I think I have a change of heart about the clock bar, I think we should hit Reading Terminal, so I can grab them extra-large shrimps and some asparagus.

"No, we're going to Macy's fat ass. You act just like a fat nigga sometimes I tell you."

Women, women, women… Can't live with them, can't live without them.

After circling the block numerous times looking for a parking spot, finally we got one.

"Come on Amin, let's catch Macy's before they close."

ONE HOUR LATER

Before I get the chance to get out my truck a van pulls up and two men gets out rushing straight for me holding some papers. I look for Tina and Tina is still getting into a parking spot five spots down and fuck, my gun is in her car.

"Hey sir, I'm looking for…

In a blink of an eye, he stabs me in my neck with a needle, injecting me with some fluid that instantly made me drowsy. I try to get out the truck, but fall face first onto a parked car. But damn, as cautious as you try to be, there's always somebody paying you more attention than you are. As I lay weak and can't move I visualize Tina coming to truck to see something's wrong and went wrong fast.

"Come on please answer this damn phone, oh my god please pick up."

"Hello?"

"Ms. Pearl, did Amin call you?"

"No, Tina just tell me my nightmare please."

"Ms. Pearl I think Amin just got Kidnapped."

"Oh, Shit I knew something was coming behind that bullshit. Hassan told me, I just knew it, I felt that shit in the bottom of my stomach, so now what Tina?'

"I don't know Ms. Pearl, but I'm thinking it's because of me when I killed a couple of their boys when we were out there in California. It was either us or them; all because we were exposed to their well-hidden secret drug lab.

Life on the Run

"Oh damn, I see it clear now. Tina these folks got Cartels in every country. Hassan is dealing with some powerful people, and they got the courts under a certain amount of control. I'm talking about judges, district attorneys; but they favor Hassan because he makes deals with niggas on death row waiting to die and he get their appeals overturned so they can get out to go overseas to work for this Cartel. Hassan's compensation for that is unknown, but shit Tina I don't know, I just don't know."

Damn I don't see me getting no sleep no time soon. I guess I'm about to start hearing all kinds of weird noises while I'm in this big ass mansion all by myself. Damn baby, please, please, please make it back home to me.

As I ease back into my senses, the first thing I realize is that I am not home. I'm stretched out on a metal operating table with four Arabians standing over top of me with white torn pieces of sheets wrapped around their mouths, as a long cut on my right shoulder is being stitched up, and the more conscious I become, the more paranoid I get, because I'm hearing more than one voice screaming from the top of their lungs from down the hallway. My fast thinking is already telling me that it's a good possibility that they're not going to kill me because why should they care so much about my arm being stitched up? Shit how did it get cut?

"Ok buddy your all set but unfortunately, you're not free to go. You killed two of my best men. You took loyalty from our organization. You put men that I took out the way back on the front line and after all you pissed me the fuck off. Oh, and I have some pretty girls here too. You do like pretty girls am I correct?"

"No"

"Well I have a special one just for you, she has HIV. If I find that you're here with us a little past your check out time we'll just get started with her showing you a nice time while we record it and send the video to our boy Hassan.

I want to cuss this funny looking ass Arabian out bad as hell but there's no telling what he'll do. They do some crazy shit to people. Then I forgot, they chop nigga's heads off and celebrate like it's Christmas or New Year's or some shit. So, I guess I'll act stupid, like I'm a little kid in a big business.

They're rolling me through an old historic dusty tunnel where the screams get louder and louder. Damn, somebody is getting tortured and the screams sounds like that shit is very painful. Fuck that! They can just kill me because shit, this is crazy. I wonder what my baby is doing? I know she's replaying that one time I held her in my arms over and over. I know Tina is wondering where I am, like I am right now, I don't have a clue where I am, from the looks of this place I know I'm far away from home.

They're rolling me into a room where it's one of their buddies already in the room looking at me with the evil eyes. I guess I'm about to get fucked up. The transporters leave, locking us in the room together. Now what type of shit is this?

My roommate walks over to me head down, looking through his keys to release me from this metal operating table. After I'm free, he sticks his hand out for a shake. I've never been this confused in my life.

"Amin, right?"

"Yes, that's me."

"My name is Tazim. I guess I'll be doing the baby sitting for a min. At first, I thought they overdosed you because you wouldn't wake up. I thought you went into a coma or something but I guess you're ok."

"Hell no, I'm not ok. I don't even know where I am."

Life on the Run

"You're in New Mexico the home base of the Cartels."

"Shit, how the hell I get over here?'

"These people are famous for underground tunnels but it's no telling how they got you pass the border. They have an inside man for everything they want to do and if they don't cooperate, then they'll start killing their families and kidnapping their kids, raping them and then sell them. You are aware that this is the home of human trafficking, right?"

"Well, what the fuck they got me for?"

"They want some type of compensation for their boys getting killed and if your boss comes up short, you would probably never see home again."

"Why you say that? They would kill me?"

"No, they would make you work for them. They already feel that your boss is not corresponding the way he should, so they're basically preparing you for these streets. They chipped your shoulder with a tracking device, so they can find you. No matter where you try to hide and if you don't have a strong organization backing you up, then you might as well get comfortable here. I think they might want you to work for them since you're already interested in the career."

"Well I noticed that you're really communicating with me, so what's your story on your position here?"

"Ok…I'm from Brooklyn New York, mom & dad separated due to my father's affiliation with his life of crime. My mom found a new boyfriend, so my father stopped helping her. As time went on the new boyfriend couldn't afford the lifestyle my mother was used to and bounced. He was a good person but my mom would get drunk, then tell him about what he was really good for. Mom started writing checks and cashing them to maintain our lavish way of living but ended up in a deeper situation that she imagined. The Citizens Bank was on a look out for her without her knowing, so when she went to try to withdraw money they stalled her, then tried to arrest her but, mom whipped out her lil .32 and started shooting everything that got in her way. Even the people that was trying to get out her way. She killed three security guards and wounded six innocent people. Right now, she's serving two life sentences. I moved in with my dad and immediately received an ultimatum which was go to school or join him in his life of crime. So, I registered for school and came out with a Master's Degree in Aviation. Right before I graduated my father moved this woman, Khaliah in with us. She was rare and beautiful. I never seen a woman that beautiful. She was half Puerto Rican and part Asian, but if you see the ass she had you would've thought he found this bitch in Africa. I started checking her out when he denied special relations and gave up a good Samaritan story. He left us alone a lot due to his responsibilities in the streets. His absence allowed enough time for me to figure out that, she was only three years older than me, I couldn't stop us from getting closer than friends. Then she started wearing tight clothing that defined her figure to the max. I would act like I didn't notice till one day, I'm researching jobs on my laptop and she stood over top of me and spilled her cherry Kool-Aid down in my V.I.P section, then reached down and grabbed me like she was about to sing a Whitney Houston song. She really grabbed my shit and complimented me. I sat there in disbelief. My father calls my phone and tells me where to find some cash in the house and that he's about to go on a seven-day business cruise. I had him on speaker so she heard everything. Khaliah goes upstairs, hops in the shower, then comes downstairs looking like she's ready for a photo shoot. With everything I had, I tried to avoid her, we started drinking liquor and listening to music, then I find that she had a problem, she couldn't keep her hands to herself. After a couple of hours go by, I ended up letting her convince me into taking half of an ecstasy pill. Moments later, here she goes with her hands going down my pants, telling me that she wonders what I taste like. In the blink of an eye, we were having some serious sex. We were hugging and tongue kissing, while I was fucking the shit out of her. It had to be something in that ecstasy pill because I was pass sexually aroused. I fucked her for almost two hours straight. She screamed so much till she started losing her voice. I bust a nut then I glanced down at my phone and noticed I had fourteen missed calls and before I can catch my breath the bedroom door opens and it's my dad looking at us with extreme hate in his face. I knew he was fucking her. He held us hostage at gun point. He missed his business cruise and everything. I just knew I was about to die. He got on the phone and started speaking another language. Then moments later, six masked men came in with guns aimed at me and Khalilah. My dad walked out the room, then the masked men blindfolded us. All I felt was a long needle going into my arm. When I woke up Khalilah, was gone and I was here on that same operating table you found yourself on. But I know a way out. When they traffic mass amounts of drugs they use boats, man-made submarines and planes and I know how to fly. All I need to know is which plane runs the best. It's four of us on this escape plan, you can make five if you didn't already make yourself at home."

"Wow, so you're a hostage Tazim?"

"Basically, I guess this was my dad's only option besides killing me. I'm gaining their trust here so it won't be long before I'm in the sky flying one of dem planes going back home."

"Well I'm in just tell me what I need to do."

"Ok, but when I get us out of here, I'm going to be homeless. Can you help me after we break free?"

"Most definitely, I will buy you your own home."

"Well if your serious, I can make this happen sooner than I thought because that's been the hold up. I been trying to figure out how will I survive and where would I live before I escaped. It's sad to say, but I'm glad you came, but I have one question?"

"And your question is?"

"Are you ready Amin

"Let's go.

To Be Continued...

Life on the Run

www.ingramcontent.com/pod-product-compliance
Lightning Source LLC
Chambersburg PA
CBHW051838020726
47502CB00005B/1853